THE LOST CHORD

A NOVEL BY
JONATHAN GOLDMAN

This book is a work of fiction. Names, characters, places and incidents are products of the author's imagination or are used fictitiously. Any resemblance to actual events or locales or person, living or dead, is entirely coincidental.

Copyright © 1999 by Jonathan Goldman

All rights reserved. No part of this book may be reproduced or utilized in any means, electronic or mechanical without prior permission in writing from the publisher, except for brief quotations embodied in critical articles and reviews.

Spirit Music, Inc.
P.O. Box 2240, Boulder, CO 80306 USA
(303) 443-8181

Jonathan Goldman's website:
www.healingsounds.com

Art Direction by Chad Darnell
Cover & graphics by Tom Rome
Angel illustration by Don Beaman
Layout assistance by Jay Nelson
Back cover photo by Sharon Dawn Gandy
Printed in the U.S.A.

First Printing: June 1999
Library of Congress Catalog Card Number: 99-93966
ISBN: 0-9748776-1-9

"Blues was the Lost Chord which, when found by a music publisher in 1903, became the Song of the 20th Century."

liner notes by Michael Fairchild
from the album *Jimi Hendrix: Blues*

The Lost Chord is dedicated to the loving
memory of Rose and Irving Goldman.

ACKNOWLEDGEMENTS

I would like to thank those who contributed to the creation of this book; Karen Anderson for her first draft editing, Don Beaman for his visionary artwork and wisdom, Sarah Benson for her healing heart and initiatory sounds, Lenny Bruce for his humor, Chad Darnell for his graphic assistance, Ray Featherman for his character and sincerity, Sharon Dawn Gandy for her ability to capture an essence, Joshua Goldman for the gift of his being, Jimi Hendrix for his purple ray sonics, Kitaro for his music and consciousness, Lauren Maddison for her back cover assistance, Jay Nelson for his help with the layout design, Tom Rome for his graphic design, Sandy Satterwhite for her publishing assistance, Shamael for his supervision, Jimmy Twyman for his encouragement and all the masters of Light, Love and Sound who have assisted with this project.

Special thanks to Andi Hilgert for her meticulous editing, support, laughter, clarity, and extraordinary love—this could not have happened without you!

May *The Lost Chord* assist all who read it in opening to the joyous and transformational energies of sound.

INTRODUCTION

I know it sounds crazy—the Lost Chord—as though something like that could ever exist. But it does, or at least it did for a while. Until I stopped it. The Lost Chord—an idea, a concept that's been kicked around throughout history, ever since Pythagoras, maybe before. The Lost Chord—a sound that could heal and transform and more. Much more! Dream on sisters. Play on brothers. Until you find out that it's real and that it's got you.

The first music was probably an attempt at healing, or at least of communicating with the spirits. When Og the Caveman picked up a stone and began to beat a rhythm on a log, probably grunting some unknown chant, it was likely that he was actually trying to talk with the Gods; maybe asking for a healing for himself and his family, or hoping for a little rain or some animals to hunt. Later on in history, when the Hebrews and other assorted nomads began to find the Holy One, they did it through sound. Stories of healings and transformation through sound are found in the Old Testament, like the time when David cured mad King Saul of his demons by playing the harp.

In fact, if you examine the basic beliefs of most of the major traditions on this planet, you'll find a commonality in their understanding that the world was created through sound. From the Old Testament you have: "And *the Lord said 'Let there be Light'". From St. John in the New Testament, it reads: "In the beginning was the Word". From the Vedas, in the Hindu tradition, you have the statement: "In the beginning was Brahman, with whom was the Word and the Word was Brahman", which smacks of a lot of similarities to the quote from St. John. The ancients knew something that we're only beginning to understand—that sound is an extraordinarily powerful energy that really does have the ability to heal and transform.*

Of course, I didn't know any of this at the time. I'm still now only beginning to understand it. Since this episode with the Lost Chord, I've found out a lot of things. I've discovered that for a lot of musicians and mystics (many times, they're one and the same), finding the Chord was a lifelong quest that often brought them to the brink of sanity, sometimes over it. Alexander Scriabin, the early 20th century composer, was so possessed with finding the Lost Chord that he apparently went mad. I think he got rather peeved that he hadn't succeeded in finding the Chord and this just took him over the edge of sanity—the last project he was working on was an attempt to create a tone that would split the Earth in half. Supposedly, Scriabin died of an infection due to a pimple on his lip just before he completed this project. Perhaps the Gods and Goddesses were not ready for such an artistic statement as the destruction of this planet. Or perhaps he should have been more patient and looked a bit longer for the Lost Chord.

Rumor had it that Pythagoras, the Greek Father of Geometry, found the Lost Chord. He had a school on the island of Krotona in the 6th century B.C. that taught three levels of initiation. The first level learned about the magic of numbers. The second level was one of purifica-

tion. At the third level, the initiates learned of the power of sound to heal and transform. They learned of the effects of different scales and modes and how to use these to elicit different physical, emotional and mental states.

Here's a story about Pythagoras. I don't know if it's true or not, but different versions of it have survived. One day Pythagoras was walking down the street with one of his students when he saw a man in an obvious state of fury, setting wood around his house. Trapped inside was this man's wife and her lover. The cuckolded husband was about to set fire to the wood, when Pythagoras instructed his student to begin playing a particular tune on his instrument. Almost immediately, the man became entranced and walked away, leaving his wife and her lover to escape.

This story illustrates just how refined the ancient knowledge of sound to change consciousness might have been. Pythagoras was said to have received much of his training of the ancient mysteries from the Egyptians, who were extremely advanced in their knowledge of sound. Some sources even claim that the pyramids were levitated and built by sound. This wouldn't surprise me one bit considering what I've recently gone through.

Poor Pythagoras. He should have used his power of sound for himself, because, according to legend, his school burned down with him in it. Maybe he didn't care anymore, or maybe he just couldn't remember what the right tune was. Regardless, whatever knowledge Pythagoras might have given to the Western world about sound for transformation and healing, perished in the flames, along with the ancient master. The same thing is probably true about much of the information about sound and other forms of vibrational energy when the Library of Alexandria was burned.

Throughout the history of the world legends and myths survive about the power of sound: from China, from India, from Tibet, from Egypt, from Israel, from Athens, from Rome, from Africa, from Australia, from South America, and from our own Native American Indians. Great legends and myths— stories about terminal illnesses being cured, legends of Gods and Goddesses coming down from the heavens for visitations and miracles, tales of extraordinary feats occurring through sound and music; dematerialization, levitation, teleportation— you name it, there's a story about it. Unfortunately, they're just stories. If the Tibetans really have a mantra that allows them to teleport across time and space, it's not something they're about to make public. Besides, who would believe it? I certainly would not have, at least not until now.

There are even stories that Adolph Hitler knew about using sound to control people. Now I might have believed this information beforehand, simply because you've got to ask yourself, how did that madman really influence so many people. Some years ago, I came across a quote in Omni *magazine that was attributed to Hitler. Here it is: "We would not have conquered Germany without the automobile, the airplane or the loudspeaker." The loudspeaker! Sound! I've since heard that Hitler worked with some nasty magicians who knew about the ability of sound to control brain waves—things that we're only now just beginning to scientifically discover. This also makes sense, in light of my Lost Chord adventure.*

I don't want to frighten you with this last bit of information, but it's something you've got to be aware of—the power of sound! I now know for a fact that sound can be used to do amazing things, things I never dreamed of before. Here's another quote, this one from the head-

lines of The New York Times *Science Section:* "*Sound shaped into dazzling new tool—can make, break or rearrange molecular structure and levitate objects!*" We're talking about an energy that can actually change matter. The uses of the power of sound are practically limitless. And the potential good that can be created is awesome. But remember that anything which can be used as a positive and transformative tool can also be utilized in its opposite form. And that is the case with this story.

The Lost Chord has remained a mystery. Undiscovered. Unfound. Stories continue to surface about its supposed discovery and then its ultimate disappearance. I think the rock group, the Moody Blues, was looking for it. Last rumor was that Jimi Hendrix had found it just before his untimely demise. But in reality, the Lost Chord, that special set of frequencies that has worked as a sonic hallucinogenic and could create interdimensional gateways, never made it past the storybooks. Until now. If Hitler had some ability to control the masses with sound, I shudder to think what he would have done with the technologies now available. Or maybe I don't have to think too much because I already know.

And if parts of this story strike you as a fairy tale, that's okay. I was in much the same position. Sometimes the mind refuses to believe those things that don't fit into our preconditioned way of thinking. Sometimes it's easier just to close our eyes and our ears to the truth. But I can't do that anymore. Not now. Not after all I've been through. I've got to tell this story. It's too important not to. And I've got to start somewhere, so I'll start at what was the beginning of this amazing adventure for me.

Christopher Shade
Boulder, Colorado

CHAPTER 1

I was sitting in the Dugout nursing a beer, when Dave finally came in.

"You missed sound check!" I said in a loud voice. I was angry and concerned. Sound check was at three-thirty. It was now close to five. The rest of the band had left a half hour before, but since Dave was my best friend, I waited around to see what had happened.

"I'm sorry," he said, wiping a greasy hand through his greasy hair. Dave is a brilliant human, maybe the smartest person I know. Besides being a great keyboard player, he is one hell of a computer wizard. But in terms of personal hygiene, he scores pretty low. This is difficult for me to understand, since he is a vegetarian. Maybe the two have nothing in common.

I took a swig of beer as Dave sat next to me at the bar. "Perrier!" he told the bartender. The bartender gave me a puzzled look. I shrugged my shoulders and took another swig of beer.

"How come you're late?" I asked. "You're never late. I think this is the first sound check you've missed in the last three years. What's the story?"

"You won't believe this, Shade," he said.

Shade, incidentally is my name. Christopher Shade. But everyone calls me Shade. Of course, Shade is not my real name. My real last name is Horowitz. But Christopher Horowitz makes for a lousy stage name, especially when you're a fiery lead guitarist. So they call me Shade.

"What won't I believe?" I asked back.

"I was over at Rusty's," Dave began. I nodded. Rusty was another computer wiz and a friend of Dave's. She was also a pretty good synthesizer player and I jammed with her on occasion. She wasn't particularly into the blues—more into the techno-pop and electronic stuff. So she didn't play with us and that was alright. "She's finally come up with it," Dave continued.

"Up with what?" I fed back. "A way to make love to computers?" Rusty was celibate as far as I could tell. I think she preferred the company of machines to those of humans, or at least of men. Anyway, that's what I had experienced.

"No man," Dave said, looking at me with a bit of disgust. "I'm serious. She finally did it."

"Did what?" I asked, trying to adopt a serious attitude to match Dave's. I drained my beer and looked at him. "What did she finally do? What did she finally come up with?"

Dave looked around and scratched his beard. For a moment I wondered if he was deciding whether to tell me or not. He peered around the Dugout, which was empty, except for the two of us and the bartender. Then he said in a low voice, "The Lost Chord, Shade. It's astounding. She found the Lost Chord."

My mouth dropped open. "What?" I exclaimed, in a very loud voice.

Dave motioned for me to keep my voice down.

"Quiet Shade, this is very important."

"You're kidding me, right?" I asked and signaled for the bartender to bring me another beer. My limit was usually one in the afternoon. I didn't want to get too nodded out before a gig, but if what Dave was telling me were true, I needed another beer.

"No, I'm quite serious. She finally did it. My good friend and super synth player and mad woman, Rusty Fox, has finally found the Lost Chord. It's true, Shade. She actually did it. It's unbelievable." Dave set down his Perrier and waited for a response from me. I was speechless.

The Lost Chord was legend and I knew it. The whole subject is not my area of expertise, but this is as much as I know. There are certain people, like Dave and particularly like Rusty, who were into what could be called a new science of sound. They were into understanding how sound affects the body and the mind. I was basically into just playing the blues, but these other people, they wanted to know more. Especially Rusty.

Now according to Rusty, as translated to me via Dave, this idea to consciously understand how to use sound to affect the body and the mind was really quite ancient. Dave told me that Pythagoras, who I remembered from high school as being the Father of Geometry, was actually a master musician. He knew how to heal with sound. I know it sounds a bit ridiculous, but why not? We all know that music can make you feel better. That's why I play the blues. And John Lee Hooker had that album about the blues being *The Healer*. So why couldn't music be used to really heal?

Dave had told me long ago that Rusty was into finding the Lost Chord. Now I had no idea what the Lost Chord was when he first mentioned it to me. I thought that maybe the Chord was the missing link between my guitar and my amplifier. I still wasn't too clear on it now, though I did have some understanding due to my association with Dave.

One night at about three o'clock in the morning, over coffee after a gig, Dave had explained to me for the first time about the Lost Chord. This mythical sound was a concept that a number of mystical musicians and composers like Scriabin had dedicated their lives to finding. It supposedly was a chordal structure that would have the ability to heal and transform.

"Well, couldn't any chord or music do that?" I had asked at the time.

"Yes," Dave had answered. "Any music could potentially help anyone depending upon the time and the place and the need of the individual. But it's pretty much hit or miss. What we're talking about here are specific sounds that would affect everyone the same way."

"I don't know if that's possible, Dave," I had told him, right before I bit into a mouthful of coffee soaked donut.

"I don't know if it is either, Shade," he had answered. "But I think if anyone's going to find the Lost Chord, it's going to be Rusty. She's obsessed with it."

Now, that conversation must have gone back at least three years. And since that time, due to my hanging out with Dave, I had found out a little more about the effects of music on the body and the mind. I'd even looked at a book or two on the subject. The more I knew, the more I was sure that the Lost Chord was impossible. And yet here was Dave, very seriously telling me that Rusty had found the Lost Chord.

"What do you mean Rusty's found the Lost Chord?" I asked.

"It's true Shade. I went over to see her right before I came here. There was plenty of time for me to make sound check. It was only two o' clock," Dave began.

"So?"

"I walk into her sound lab where she's incredibly excited about having found the Lost Chord. Like you, I'm a bit of a skeptic. So I said 'Show me!' Only, of course, you can't look at the Lost Chord. You've got to hear it. So I put on headphones and she turned on her computer and synthesizer, and suddenly wham! I'm out of it."

"Are you sure she didn't feed you some of that wacky weed?" I asked.

"Cut it out Shade," Dave said defensively. "I'm serious. Rusty turned on the synthesizer, put some program into it, played some sounds, and the next thing I knew it was a couple of hours later."

"What?" I shouted.

"I'm not kidding."

"What happened?" I asked. "Did you go unconscious?"

"I don't know," Dave replied. "It was as though I suddenly wasn't there. The sound started happening and then I was out of my body, zooming through the universe. It was amazing."

"I'll bet," I said.

"I didn't want to come back. It was so beautiful."

"Wait a minute," I said. "You mean you were out of your body or unconscious for two hours?"

"That's right," he said.

"And that's why you missed sound check?"

"That's right," he said.

"Then why didn't Rusty stop playing that sound, the

Lost Chord so you could come back to your body and make it to sound check?" It was obvious that at the time I had not grasped the full significance of the situation.

"No, you don't understand," Dave explained. "She wasn't subjecting me to the sound all that time. She only played the Chord for about five minutes. It took her the rest of the time to get me conscious again. And then more time after that to get me into a condition to drive."

"That's pretty irresponsible of Rusty," I said, still not grasping the situation. I drained the rest of my second beer, which could have been a contributing factor to the thickness of my mind at the time.

"She didn't know what it would do," Dave defended her. "She had no idea what it's effect would be or how long it would last. She had only discovered the Lost Chord yesterday. It's not her fault. After her, I was the first person to try it."

"Let me get this straight," I said, trying to sum up the situation. "Rusty discovers the Lost Chord. Then she tries it on you. She plays it for five minutes and it knocks you out for two hours?"

Dave shook his head. "It didn't really knock me out Shade. It put me out of my body. It was like nothing I have ever experienced. I was fully consciousness. I have complete memory of the entire experience. I was zooming around the universe in what felt like my physical body, though I know it wasn't. It was really real! I spent time on Mars and the asteroids. It was outrageous."

"This is very hard to swallow," I said. "I have all the faith in the power of sound to do some radical things, but it strikes me that maybe you were dosed with something and didn't know about it. Maybe Rusty slipped something into your Perrier before she put on the sound."

"Maybe Shade," Dave admitted. "But I don't think so. I think she somehow has discovered something that is pretty amazing. Maybe even mind blowing!"

"If she has discovered the Lost Chord, Dave my friend, she may have discovered something that could change the world."

"I think she did Shade. I think she did." Dave said adamantly.

I got up off the bar stool. "Can you drive?" I asked. My vehicle was parked around back and I didn't feel like moving it.

"How do you think I got here?" Dave asked.

"Then let's be off."

"Where?" he asked.

"To pay your friend Rusty a visit. We don't have to be back here to play for another three hours. If she really has discovered the Lost Chord, I want to be the next person who gets a chance at experiencing it."

And we were off.

CHAPTER 2

First and foremost, it might appear that I am really ignorant about understanding sound. This is not correct. I think sometimes in the name of my rock n' roll guise, I tend to project an image that is somewhat less than bright— in fact, an image at times of a paleolithic troglodyte. But, it's not true.

In reality, I am actually a teacher. Not only do I teach guitar, but I also teach classes on music theory and occasionally music history. Difficult as it may be to believe, I have a bachelors degree in English and even did some graduate work in journalism. I have always loved playing music, even back in high school when I performed in my first rock band. And through the years, I have had some minor successes in the music field, at least locally.

The reality base, however, is that I'm now 33. And there's nothing worse or more depressing than an aging aspiring rock star. I gave up my dreams of becoming a household word, like Prince or the Beatles years ago. This was when I began teaching. There were a number of reasons for this. First, it allowed me to bring in money on a consistent basis. Playing in clubs and other venues is sporadic. Sometimes the gigs are there and sometimes they're not. Second, the older I became, the less glamourous it was to be on the road.

I remember when I was in my early 20's, the idea of touring around with a band was thrilling. I had the opportunity of getting paid to play music, and living the rock n' roll lifestyle. You know, complete with sex and drugs and all that good stuff. It was actually pretty wonderful for a while, but about five years ago, as old B.B. King once let us know, the thrill was gone. I was playing in an original rock band called the Silencers and we were traveling all around New England. We never made it much further than that, but we had a good local following. Unfortunately, I had, more or less, a substance abuse problem, and the older I got, the more I abused substances. I remember passing out on stage a couple of times, which was really uncool. And now as I think back, I must have been pretty unhappy to have reached that level of life.

I was tired of the constant late nights and traveling; never being in the same city or even the same bed twice in a row. Most importantly, my health was beginning to deteriorate. My liver was starting to trouble me; I had to stop drinking and smoking and doing other kinds of intoxicants if I wanted to make it to the future. At least that was what the doctors told me and I tended to agree, considering the condition of my body at the time.

You know, it's pretty strange how things catch up with you. Both my parents were alcoholics. I think that maybe it ran in the family. I'm not talking about just drinking beer either. I'm talking about the hard stuff: scotch, rum, vodka, gin and all those things that make you feel so good—at least for a while.

Anyway, I remember waking up one morning in

incredible pain. It felt like my belly was about to explode. I went to see a doctor and found out that, not only did I have an ulcer, I was also on my way to the cemetery fast if I didn't clean up my act. Which I did.

Actually, it wasn't that difficult. Part of my ability to change lifestyles was based on the fact that there was a woman who dearly loved me and assisted me in giving up alcohol, tobacco and drugs. I also gave up rock n' roll. At least temporarily.

This woman, who called herself Star Flower, stayed with me for two years. She assisted me in staying off the toxic substances, gave me hope for living, and was basically an extraordinary angel to a suffering soul. Then, one morning, I woke up and she was gone. Except for the changes in myself, it was as though she had never been there. I'd go more heavily into detail about this, but it's too painful. Sometimes, I even wonder if she was ever there to begin with. But I know that due to her love and wisdom, I became a changed man.

As I said, I stayed off rock n' roll for a while. About two years, actually, until Star Flower left me. After that, I was in such great pain that I had to either start playing music again, or start hitting the bottle. Before that, I figured you couldn't have one without the other, alcohol and music. But somehow, when Star Flower left me, I knew deep down in my soul, that I could begin playing music again without using all those substances that were killing me.

So music came back into my life. To be exact, it was the blues that I turned to for solace and comfort. And if my rock n' roll playing had been screaming with anger, my blues playing was fiery with pain and sadness. It was beautiful and it helped fill the hole in my heart from the loss of my lady.

I began to teach guitar privately, and then sometimes substituted in schools. I found that it wasn't so bad. And what's more, I discovered that there were aspects of teaching that I really liked. I was almost as good a teacher as I was a guitar player. And frankly, there were more guitar players around than teachers. So I began to focus my work on teaching. Mainly, I substitute whenever I can. I like it that way. It allows me to continue playing music and at the same time to experience other aspects of life. What I have created for myself is the ability to play music in a band about three nights a week, teach guitar to half a dozen different students and substitute teach one to three days a week. It works well for me.

I also began playing the blues. I began playing in bands that played locally; first in Boston where I had been living and then later on, here in Boulder. The Cosmic Blues Band is what I called the group I now play in. We formed after I moved to Boulder, five years ago. There was Dave on keyboards, Bill on bass and Tony on drums. We were pretty good. And we became the house band at the Dugout. We usually end up playing two or three nights a week. It works out fine. All four of us have other gigs. Dave is a computer geek. He develops software programs for companies. Tony works as a social worker. He's a very gentle man who truly enjoys helping people. Bill is an artist who occasionally has showings of his work. It's not bad really; looks a bit like Escher's, only not quite as good. But he's always improving.

Boulder is a very interesting place. I moved here from Boston, where I went to college and then subsequently played music. I moved because of a woman. It wasn't Star Flower, but someone else who helped fill the gap in my heart created by Star Flower. Her name was

Ellen and she was a school teacher and a skier. Sometime during the summer of 1994, she realized that she would rather ski than teach in the Newton Public School system and decided to move to the Rocky Mountains. We were living together and I had spent a lot of time in Boston myself—over 10 years, in fact—ever since I started B.U. A change of location did not seem like such a bad idea. So, I followed her out to Boulder, and we set up house together. Six months later, I left her and the apartment we had been renting because I found out that she had been dating a ski instructor on the side. Actually, I caught the two of them in bed together. It was not a pleasant sight and was more than I could handle. She ended up living with the ski instructor and I ended up renting a room on Mapleton. I've been there ever since. It's really not too bad. The rent is inexpensive. It's close to the center of town. And thus far, I haven't met a woman I can bear to be with for more than a short time. But perhaps this will change.

I hate to admit it, but women have dictated my entire life. A woman was responsible for bringing me into this world. Women have been responsible for most of my major decisions in the world. And, probably, I will leave this planet because of a woman. Did I mention that Rusty Fox who discovered the Lost Chord was a woman? And a fine keyboard player? Did I tell you I'd had a crush on her ever since I met her through Dave? Did I tell you she had beautiful red hair and a face like a cherub? Did I tell you her body was firm and tight and that I would often get aroused by being around her? Did I tell you she thinks I am a dork and doesn't want anything to do with me? Ah yes, Rusty. I tried every maneuver in the book to get her to like me. Our jamming together was incredible. Fluid. Rhythmic. We'd shifts keys at the same time, change frequencies as though two souls were playing as one. I just know that if we had the opportunity, we could literally make beautiful music together. But I've never had the opportunity and doubt I ever will.

I think the problem may be that Rusty is spiritually oriented and I'm not. Sure, I've done a bit of exploration into the mystical. You can't really help doing that here in Boulder, which is the capital of New Age consciousness. There are more health food restaurants than McDonalds here, and every other person wears a crystal and talks about past lives.

After Ellen threw me out, I attended a number of different lectures and workshops that were spiritually oriented. I was in this burg, and given its propensity toward New Age activities, I thought it would be a great place to meet women. I did one workshop on meditation. Another workshop on healing. Another workshop on meeting your soul mate (I thought for sure this would be one where I'd find someone to take home), but somehow, the New Age never clicked with me. I was too much of what used to be commonly referred to as a male chauvinist. That's not really true. I'm not and I don't think I've ever been called that. But on a subtle level, I think that's what a lot of women, particularly women in Boulder, think of me.

It's just that I operate from what they call the root chakra. It's part of what is mystically termed the esoteric anatomy. These chakras are energy centers that are associated with different parts of the body. There are seven chakras in all. The top is the crown chakra, located at the top of the head. It's the highest and I guess most people think the best. It's a very spiritual center. If you've ever seen pictures of saints and other holy beings with halos around their head, that's a depiction of an activated crown chakra. There is also a chakra in the forehead—that one's often called the third eye—then a chakra at the throat, one in the center of the chest called the heart chakra, a chakra at the navel area, a chakra a few inches below that and then my favorite, the root chakra, located in the genital region. Quite frankly, I don't even think I have a crown chakra, or if I do, I'm not aware of it. I do, however, have an activated root chakra. That's the lowest chakra. The sexual chakra. Or at least I think it is. All I know for sure is that my sexual chakra is quite nicely in motion all the time, thank you.

It's not that I think about sex all the time; it's just that when I'm around women, I do think about sex. And I admit that I often act on it, too. And once again, I guess, not so subtly. What the hell. I like sex. I believe that it's possible to have a really good time without doing anybody any harm. So I put out a lot of sexual energy. Especially when I'm around women. And I guess that's why I never did too well with the females in those workshops. It just was not a very good mix.

I have a friend named Nick who often goes to various New Age events and seems to do very well finding women to relate to. He's told me that I need to become more sensitive—more loving and open. I don't really understand what he's talking about, but perhaps that is part of the problem. I'm just trying to be who I am, and perhaps that's just not right for Boulder. Sometimes I think that I should contemplate moving to a place like L.A., or back to New York where I originally came from. In those places sex and drugs and rock n' roll are still accepted as a viable consciousness.

But I wasn't in L.A. or New York. I was in Boulder, driving down Canyon Blvd. with Dave, on the way to see Rusty. And I was really excited. I was trying to figure out if I was excited because I was going to see Rusty, or because there was the remotest possibility that she had discovered the Lost Chord.

Rusty lived in a two bedroom condo on the corner of 18th and Canyon. I don't really know how she afforded it. She worked occasionally as a computer consultant, but most of the her time was spent working with her home recording unit and trying to discover the Lost Chord. I think she was one of those independently wealthy people you always wish you were. Her last name was Fox. I'd heard rumors that she was related to 20th Century Fox. But you never know. We'd never gotten close enough for me to ask.

Anyway, enough of this autobiographic material. It doesn't do me any good thinking about it. And it doesn't do you much good. The thing about past memories is that they're useful when they're good, and not so useful when they're not.

Dave and I didn't speak much during the ride over to Rusty's. I was caught up in too many flashbacks about my life. It happens sometimes. He and I had been friends now for too many years to make conversation a necessity. This allowed me to obsess about my past. Thinking about my past is something I feel immensely uncomfortable doing, but still somehow enjoy it. I shudder to think what this means.

We sat in silence during the 5 minute ride from the Dugout, which was on Pearl and 10th, to Rusty's condo. Then, we were out of the car and standing at her front door.

I tried to straighten myself out, tucking in my shirt and smoothing out whatever disheveled parts of me needed fixing in order to help my appearance. Not that it mattered. I could have been wearing a tux and a top hat and it wouldn't have impressed Rusty. I think maybe she was beyond impressing—at least from me. The woman did not like me and there was no way getting around it. I hadn't paid a visit to her in a long time, probably six months or more. And I wouldn't have been paying her a visit now except for the seemingly exceptional experience that Dave had just had. I needed to find out what was going on and so I was there. But I felt uncomfortable and there was no way around it.

Still, I was the one who rang her doorbell, and I was the one she would see first. I took a deep breath and waited for the worst. Then Rusty answered the door.

CHAPTER 3

The front door swung open and there she was, dressed in a turquoise flannel shirt and jeans. Rusty Fox looked me up and down for a brief moment. I was afraid she was going to slam the door in my face. Then she saw Dave and broke into a smile.

"Back so soon?" she asked, addressing the question to Dave as she opened the door wider.

"Hello, Rusty," I said, still standing in the cold outside.

"Hello, Shade," she said coldly.

"Can we come in?" I asked.

"He can," she said. "You can if you must." She gestured for us to come inside.

Dave and I walked into her place. It hadn't changed much since the last time I was there. Her living room was filled with computers, synthesizers, speakers and other equipment. There was a couch at the far corner, which I made my way to, avoiding the various instruments, designed no doubt as an obstacle course for anyone in the vicinity. Dave followed me. We both sat together on the couch while Rusty adjusted herself at a stool in front of one of her synthesizers.

"What can I do for you?" she asked in a pleasant

tone addressed to Dave.

"You tell me," I said. "Old Dave here showed up an hour late for sound check and proceeded to tell me that he was blasted into oblivion by some 'lost chord' that you had discovered."

Rusty remained cool and ignored my statement. "How are you doing, David?" she asked. She always called him David, not Dave. I think it was a sign of respect for his scientific mind. She always called me Shade, never Christopher.

Dave looked at her and smiled. "I'm doing fine now, Rusty. But you know, I really was some place else during those sounds."

Rusty's tone turned somber. "Yes, I know David. I was worried about you for a while."

"What do you mean worried?" I asked, as pleasantly as I could.

Finally she acknowledged me and responded to my question. "I subjected David to the frequencies for only a few minutes. He was in a really deep Delta state for over an hour after that. I was afraid I was going to have to call an ambulance or take him to the emergency room at Boulder Community Hospital. Thank God, David finally came out of it."

I had hung around Dave, Rusty, and others working with sound long enough to know that she was talking about the Delta brain wave state. There are four primary frequency band widths that the brain operates within. The brain pulses and vibrates at frequencies between 1/2 to 25 cycles per second. This way of measuring brain wave activity, cycles per second, or hertz as it's called scientifically, is the same measurement that's given to sound. The most common frequency range of brain wave activity is called Beta. This is between about 13 and 25 cycles per second. This is the frequency range that the brain normally operates at when we are engaged in our regular day to day activity: working, playing—that sort of thing. The next frequency range is called Alpha, and it is between 7 and 13 cycles per second. This is the range of brain activity that occurs when we're daydreaming, or engaged in light meditation. It seems that the slower the brain waves operate, the deeper the altered states of consciousness will be.

Theta is the frequency range that is between about 4 and 7 cycles per second. It is found in very deep meditation. Then, there's Delta. Delta, the frequency range of the brain which Rusty had been talking about, is between 1/2 a cycle and 4 cycles per second. It's usually found in people who are comatose, or when you're in a really deep sleep that's very hard to wake from. Lately, however, I knew that scientists had found these frequencies in people doing deep healing work, as well as those interesting beings called trance channels. Rusty had said that Dave had been in this Delta state.

"How did you know he was in Delta?" I asked.

"Well, I had him hooked up to a Mind Mirror at the time," Rusty answered. A Mind Mirror was a fairly simple, though accurate instrument for measuring brain wave frequencies.

"Oh," I replied. I turned to Dave. "You didn't tell me you were hooked up."

"You didn't ask," was his clever reply. But it was true.

I looked up at Rusty. "Rusty," I began, "What the hell is going on?"

She looked at me with a cynical expression. "You

didn't know, Shade? I've been working on trying to induce different states of consciousness with sound." She pointed at her equipment around the room.

"Yeah, I know that," I sighed. "But according to Dave, you not only have been trying to create different states of consciousness, you seem to have succeeded."

"Yes," Rusty exclaimed, demonstrating a little emotion for the first time that evening. "What an extraordinary scientific breakthrough!"

"Extraordinary?" I repeated. "Maybe. But I also think it could be very dangerous."

"Nonsense," she said haughtily. "David is fine and my Lost Chord is going to change the world."

Now, may I digress for a minute and say that from my rather limited viewpoint, playing with sound to change brain wave states is both extraordinary and dangerous. The concept that sound waves could affect brain waves was proven years ago. The discovery was of a very simple phenomenon. If a frequency of, for example, 100 cycles per second is put in one ear via headphones, and a frequency of 105 cycles per second is put in the other ear, the brain will begin to vibrate to the frequency that is the difference between them. In the above illustration, the difference between 105 and 100 is 5 cycles a second. In this case, the brain would begin to vibrate at 5 cycles per second, in the lower range of Theta. Two frequencies that are slightly out of tune have the potential ability of actually changing the rhythms of the brain.

This discovery, made in the 1970's, was called "sonic entrainment". Like many other scientific breakthroughs, it was really was nothing new. The phenomenon of using sound to affect consciousness was probably quite ancient. It was certainly known about and used by sacred traditions such as the Tibetan Buddhist and aboriginal shaman. They may not have had a specific scientific understanding of this, but they knew that if they created instruments that were slightly out of tune, they could help induce altered states in the people who were listening to the sounds.

The scientific discovery of sonic entrainment has now been enhanced by researchers throughout the world trying to build a better mousetrap, or in this case, create a more powerful way of changing brain wave activity through sound. The recordings and instruments which use this technology, however, have still not been totally successful in producing a desired result. A person might listen to a recording of sounds with Theta frequencies on it and enter the Theta state of consciousness. Or they might not, depending upon the person. The reason for this is not entirely understood. It frequently takes several minutes for the person listening to these brain wave sounds to enter into an altered state. Once the sound stops, the person listening to these sounds will quickly drop back into a normal brain wave state. Usually, that is. I had also heard of people having epileptic seizures after listening to these brain wave frequencies. I considered it dangerous. I also knew that with today's technology, you did not have to use headphones. It was possible to use stereo speakers to project the sound into a room and affect people. And the sounds that were being projected did not even have to be audible. They could be subliminal, below our threshold of hearing and still affect people. This potentially bordered on brainwashing, which is not my favorite activity.

The whole thing smacked of mind control. I didn't like it one bit. To be truthful, I was glad that the use of sound to affect brain wave activity had not been all that successful. There were lots of people, particularly scientists, and that cross over breed, scientists/musicians such as Rusty, who were trying to make brain wave frequencies more effective. Until that moment, I hadn't thought that anyone had succeeded. But a feeling in my gut made me think that Rusty had indeed discovered something no one else had. I continued with my questioning.

"Rusty," I began, "What is so different about your Lost Chord from all of the other sonic entrainment devices, tapes and frequencies that are out on the market now?"

"Why the big interest in my work now, Shade?" she asked snidely. "I've been doing this research since 1988, long before you ever got to Boulder. It has been my passion for over ten years. You never asked me about it when I made the mistake of going out with you on that awful night. Why do you care now?"

Okay, so I didn't mention that I went out with Rusty once. And it was a disaster. I went with her to a lecture on quantum mechanics. I almost fell asleep. Okay, I did fall asleep, and then when I was driving her home, I tried to put the make on her and she put an elbow in my solar plexus, which was the extent of our physical contact thus far. I didn't mention it because it was truly one of the low moments in my life and I wish she hadn't brought it up.

"I'm only interested in it because of what happened to Dave. He said he listened to your sounds for five minutes and he zoomed around the galaxy for the next two hours. I'd like to try it," I admitted.

"What?" Rusty exclaimed. "You? Mr. I'm-Not-Interested-in-the-Esoteric."

"Yeah," I said again. "I'd like to try it."

"Why?" she asked. "It's not your style."

"Because I'd like to go through something like Dave did. That's why. Dave said he was fully conscious. I'd like to have that experience. Who knows, maybe it would change my life and my belief system about all of this," I explained.

"Well wouldn't that be something?" Rusty replied sarcastically. "You've been blocking things all your life Shade, and meditation and drugs don't seem to have made any difference in terms of changing your belief system or your awareness." She nodded her head, "I would like to see if my Lost Chord can make a difference."

"Great!" I said enthusiastically. "Only, I'm a little worried. How dangerous do you think it is?"

Rusty shrugged her shoulders. "I don't know Shade, but I can't be sure. After all, it's just sound waves. It's not like I'm injecting a chemical into your body. There are always potential hazards in anything," she said sarcastically. "So far, only David and I have tried the Lost Chord frequencies. I'm certainly not taking responsibility for anything that happens to you. You probably won't even experience anything anyway. But one never knows." She looked at me and smiled coyly, "Are you sure you want to try this?"

"Yeah, I'm sure," I said. I was not going to let her psyche me out. "At least I think I'm sure." I looked at my watch. It was now nearly six o'clock. "Do you think I can do this and still be in shape to play tonight?"

"I honestly don't know Shade," Rusty said in exasperation. "The sounds might send you into your future and you'd wake up having missed your precious performance at the Dugout. That certainly would be a disaster.

The world would really be reeling from a night of missing your playing in the Cosmic Blues Band. I don't know if we'd ever recover."

"Do I detect a note of sarcasm in your voice?" I asked politely. Rusty just shook her head. I looked around the room. "Okay, where is it?"

"Where's what?" she asked.

"Your Lost Chord instrument," I replied.

"Shade, if you had even bothered to find out the simplest thing about what I've been doing, you would know that the Lost Chord is not an instrument, but a computer program. It's stored on a disk in that computer." She pointed to a Mac next to her keyboard. "All I've got to do is bring up the program, have you listen to the sounds on these headphones I have for five minutes, and then see what happens."

"Are the headphones necessary?" I asked.

Rusty nodded her head. "They are, unless you want David and I to join you in dreamland. Then who would turn off the program and be there to watch you?"

"I get it," I said.

"Do you want to put on the Mind Mirror in order to monitor your brain wave activity?"

"Do you have to put gunk on the ends of those terminals and put it on my head?" I asked.

I had tried one of those brain wave monitoring instruments before. They had to apply this salve where they attach the ends of these wires to your head. It's very sticky and since I was still planning on being on stage in less than two and a half hours, I wasn't up for it messing up my hair.

"Yes," she said.

"No thanks!" I said. "I've got my image to uphold."

"God, Shade, you are so egotistical." Rusty rolled her eyes. "Well, it's fine with me if you don't want to be monitored. It's your life."

"I'm a grown man," I said.

Rusty said nothing in response to this but simply shook her head and sighed deeply. Then she got up and walked over to me with a set of headphones in her hand. They were attached to the synthesizer by a cord that was at least 20 feet long.

"Here," she said. "Put these on. I'm sorry if they'll mess up you hair."

"No problem," I looked at the couch. "Can I just sit here?" I asked.

"Fine," she said curtly. "Simply make yourself comfortable, which I'm sure will not be difficult for you."

"Anything else you want to tell me?" I said, putting on the headphones.

Rusty walked over to the computer keyboards and punched some buttons. "Bon Voyage!" was the last thing I remember her saying.

CHAPTER 4

The angel looked as real as anything I'd ever seen in my whole life. It was magnificent. Huge, glowing. With wings. And it wasn't androgynous. It was definitely male, though I didn't see any body hair on it. Beautiful flowing blond hair, but definitely male.

"Where I am?" I asked.

His voice was gentle and soft, yet at the same time loud and booming. I couldn't understand why, but I could understand the words. "You have passed through a gateway. You are now in the place beyond time and space. We have no words for this. You might call it heaven."

I looked around. I was inside some kind of extraordinary white and gleaming domed structure. "Am I dead?" I asked.

"No," the angel laughed. "You are merely visiting."

"Do you know who I am?"

"Of course, you are Christopher Horowitz. Known as Shade at this point in time and space."

"And who are you?" I asked.

"We have been called Shamael. We are the Angel of Sound," the angel replied.

I shook my head in disbelief. I didn't understand the reference to itself in the plural, but nothing was making sense to me. So I asked the obvious, "Am I asleep?" I rubbed my hands together. They felt real. Then, I tried something I'd heard about. I pinched myself. It hurt, but I didn't wake up. Then I looked down at my feet. They were there. But that didn't help. I still didn't wake up.

"No, Christopher, you are not asleep. Except in the understanding that you have been asleep since you have incarnated this time on the planet which you call Earth." Shamael smiled, "No, Christopher. You are not asleep. You are merely being awakened. This may be one of the first times that you have been awakened in a long, long while. We welcome you."

I was aware that everything around me had a luminescent glow, including me. When I looked at my hands, and at my feet too, there was also a glow around them. "This is incredible," I said. "I can't believe this is happening!"

Shamael looked at me with eyes of ancient wisdom and laughed, "It is happening, and yet it is not. You are in a multi-dimensional frame of consciousness, able to access different planes of existence. This has allowed you to experience the plane you are now on. Yet, back on the Earth plane, you are merely sitting in an upright position listening to some extraordinary sounds."

"Does everyone who listens to the Lost Chord come to this place?" I asked.

"No," Shamael said, laughing again. "The frequency that you speak of, this Lost Chord, creates a gateway or portal that allows people to access different dimensionalities, or levels of consciousness. You have been able to access this specific dimension or plane of existence. You have been granted an audience with us in particular."

"Who are you?" I asked again.

"We have told you. We are Shamael, the Angel of Sound," the being said.

I shook my head. "Yeah, but I've never heard of you. I've heard of Michael and Raphael and Gabriel, but I've never heard of Shamael."

The angel nodded. "We have not been named for many a millennium—until the time when humankind was once again ready to work with the sacredness of sound—to give voice to the angelic energies inherent in these sounds. This has happened or you would not be here."

I was awe struck. "Am I the first to make contact with you, because of the Lost Chord?"

The angel nodded. "It would appear so for it is. We have been present since the beginning, yet we have not named ourselves for many a millennium."

I was having difficulty grasping the situation. "I don't understand. Why me?"

"Because you have appeared before us, Christopher Horowitz. Is that not reason enough?"

"But why?" I asked. "I'm not spiritual. I can't even meditate. And I don't have out of body experiences or visions of heaven."

"You are here because you are meant to be here," the angel answered. "But it is good that you have feelings of unworthiness. Many great spiritual teachers and guides have felt unworthy. You are here because you have a destiny to fulfill and we can assist you in that destiny."

"Yeah," I said, "but I don't just feel unworthy. I think this is a mistake."

"It is as it should be."

"You don't understand," I said trying to explain.

Panic was beginning to set in. I didn't know where I was. I didn't know why I was. But the whole thing seemed far too real and it didn't make any sense. "You've got me all wrong," I said. "I'm not spiritual, I'm not even religious. Until a few minutes ago, I didn't think I believed in angels, or God for that matter. And if there's some important destiny to fulfill, you had better pick the right person for the job."

"You have been asleep," Shamael said. "This does not mean that you can not wake up. This is what is happening now. There is a reason for this."

"But why me?" I continued. "Why now?"

The angel put his arm on my shoulder. "Think," he said. "Think what has happened most recently to you."

"I was and am still experiencing the Lost Chord," I said. "And the Lost Chord creates a gateway that allows access to different dimensions."

"That is so." Shamael said.

"And so what?" I asked. "I don't get it."

"You are not seeing it yet, but we will help!" the angel began. "You are aware of the power of this Lost Chord, as you call it?"

"Not really. At least not until now. I never even believed that something like this could exist."

"But it does exist," the angel acknowledged. "For your friend has inadvertently discovered it. It existed once before, but knowledge of how to create it was taken away."

"Why?" I asked.

"Why do you think, Christopher?"

"Misuse? Abuse? It being used as a way of controlling others?"

The angel nodded. "Yes, that and much more. This Lost Chord is an extraordinary gift that can allow humankind great acceleration and growth to higher consciousness. Yet, it must be used wisely or its power can wreck havoc upon the planet."

"How?" I asked.

"It must be used carefully, in controlled situations, in sacred situations, in which the individual is aware of what is being done for otherwise it becomes a narcotic. This Lost Chord creates an almost instantaneous disassociation from the physical body. If it were to be used improperly without understanding and knowledge of its power, the results could be disastrous."

"You mean if it were to be broadcast over the airwaves, all the people hearing it would go unconscious?" I said, amazed that I was thinking about this.

The angel spread his wings. "Yes, that and more."

"You want me to make sure that this doesn't happen, don't you?" I asked.

"That is so!" The angel flapped his wings several times. His wingspan was enormous. Shamael stood at least 9 feet tall. His wingspan was easily 12 feet across. It was impressive. "The frequency of your Lost Chord is not new. It has been achieved in the past through the sacred chants of mantras of different traditions. But then, those that had achieved the state of consciousness necessary to create such gateways through which to travel were aware of what they were doing. This Lost Chord is an artificially created set of frequencies generated by a computer, a machine. It is different. In a way it is more powerful and therefore more dangerous. It can be used by the uneducated, the thrill seeking, the power controlling. Like anything else that has ever been created, it has its opposite use. If used properly, it can be an extraordinary tool to help assist humans in their development. We can not insist, but we must suggest that you make sure that the Lost Chord is used properly."

"How?" I asked. "And why are you always speaking in the plural?"

"You will know," the angel said. Then he took his luminescent pointer finger and tapped me in the middle of my forehead.

"What's happening?" I asked as my skull began to light up.

"It is part of your awakening!" the angel said. He flapped his wings and began to rise up in the air. I was having a difficult time keeping track of him since everything was spinning.

CHAPTER 5

I really hated this multi-dimensional stuff. One minute I was sitting comfortably on a couch in Boulder, Colorado with hardly a care in the world. The next minute I was having a heart to heart with the Angel of Sound. And then, there I was spiraling through a galaxy. Only it wasn't a galaxy. It was more! Then, I went through a tunnel. Only it wasn't round, it was diamond shaped, and as I went through, it was as though there were images, thoughts, pictures, sounds and impression being projected at me simultaneously.

I saw myself in past lives, I saw ancient civilizations and future civilizations, I saw the Pyramids being built by sound and Atlantis being destroyed by crystals. I saw the first primordial creature crawl out of the sludge and become a land dweller. I saw extraterrestrials genetically engineering apes who later became men. My past lives flashed by like cards being shuffled in a deck. I was a man, a woman, a priest, a slave. I knew Buddha and the Christ and Napoleon and Jack the Ripper. I was a musician and a warlord, a princess and a pauper. I had lived more times than I could count and I remembered every one of those lives. I saw the interconnectedness of all things, from the smallest microbes to the largest stars. I understood the sacredness of all things. I was all things and all things were me. I understood the interconnectedness of the universe, the web of existence; how all things that ever were and ever would be, had already been created; how time and space did not exist and free will created everything. There were no paradoxes here. I was omniscient. I was omnipresent. And I was conscious. It was too much for me.

A little bit of knowledge may be a dangerous thing, but this was something else. It was both frightening and exhilarating. And it was absolutely mind boggling. Even as I was absorbing and maintaining this tremendous information, knowledge and experience, I realized that I had been in a very similar place before; not frequently, but on occasion, in my younger college days, when I had taken a psycho-active drug such as LSD or mescaline. I had been in a similar space before, but back then, it had been too much for me. And it was too much for me now.

"Please! Please!" I shouted, though the words did not come out as words. They were merely thoughts. But they were being received. "Please help me!"

Suddenly I was back in the luminescent room with Shamael. "How may we assist you?"

I looked at the angel. "I am you and you are me," I was going to say; "And we are all together," but it was difficult since I was gasping for air in a place that probably was a vacuum. Everything was still spinning, especially all those images going through my head. I was still spiraling through the universe and yet still on the couch in Boulder. I was multi-dimensional and I understood multi-dimensionality. It was too much for me. "And I understand why you keep referring to yourself in the plural!"

"Indeed," Shamael said with a smile.

"Shamael—what's happened to me?"

"It is part of the awakening process. You have had it before, but you did not wish to recall it."

"I don't wish to recall now," I said. "This is too much for me. I can't take all this knowledge. Is this what enlightenment is like?"

"For some," the angel replied.

"Well, I don't want it!" I shouted. "Maybe being here with you, I can deal with it. But back on earth, I just know it would be too much for me. I couldn't function. I just couldn't exist. I can't be simultaneously aware of my actions on different planes of existence and still play guitar in a blues band. I don't want to remember all my past lives, or the future ones that I'm supposed to have. It's too much for me to handle. Can you make this go away?"

"We can do anything you desire. Do you wish complete knowledge removal, or merely partial removal? Would you prefer to be removed from this experience all together? We are here to guide you, that is all. We are not here to interfere. We do not wish to create any discomfort for you or to place you in situations which are not for the greatest development of your highest self."

"Yes, I understand," I acknowledged. "And no," I said without hesitation. "I don't want total removal of the information and experiences. Just take away enough so that I'll be able to function as my normal self."

"You are being awakened," Shamael said. "And transformation will occur because of this."

"I realize that," I said. "I know I have free will in this, and I do see my destiny. I understand. I want to assist the planet and I want to achieve my purpose. It's just the knowledge that I've just received is a little too much. Can you remove the omniscience and the total understanding of everything and the total connection to all aspects of the universe? Leave me a little bit of this and that. Maybe some past lifetime memories, and an inkling of how everything is created. Of course, I want to have a clear remembrance of this experience with you. But remove the rest. It's just too much right now."

"Is that all?" Shamael asked.

"Yes," I said. "How will I be able to contact you?"

The glow started to fade and I could feel and see and be myself spinning back through the dimensionalities, back into my body in Boulder. The last thing I heard as I reentered my body was the angel's voice saying, "We will meet again."

CHAPTER 6

I was back in my body in Boulder. There was Dave and Rusty leaning over me looking concerned. Everything was the same and yet everything was different. "I want to go back," I said. "Put the sound back on. I want to go back."

"Are you alright?" Dave asked.

I guess I must have slumped over on the couch because they were both helping me to sit up. "Wow!" was my answer. My vision was blurry and the whooshing noise that I had heard as I spun through the universe was still in my ears. I shook my head, trying to clear it. "I think so. But I want to go back. Put the Lost Chord back on. It was incredible back there. I want to go back."

Then the experience I had just had began to permeate my conscious mind. I realized what I had been through. I needed to assimilate the experience I had just had, not go for more. I took a deep breath and looked up at Dave and Rusty. "How long was I out?"

Dave looked at his watch. "It's seven forty five now. You were gone for about an hour and forty-five minutes."

"Amazing! And how long did you keep the sound on for?" I asked.

"We only gave you three minutes Shade," Rusty answered. "I didn't want you to be out for too long considering your precious gig."

"Oh God! That's right. The gig!" I exclaimed. "I don't think I can make it."

"What's the matter?" Dave asked, a worried expression on his face. "Don't you feel alright? I think it's just reentry problems. It took me about a half hour before I felt fully grounded. But don't worry, there's plenty of time to make the gig."

"No, it's not that," I said. "I went through something. Something happened. I need time to assimilate it."

"What, Shade? What?" Dave asked, rubbing his hands together. "What happened to you? Did you blast through outer space or visit any planets?"

I rubbed my face with my hands. "Got any water?" I managed to ask.

"Sure," said Rusty. It was the first time I had seen her act pleasantly to me. Or maybe it was me that was perceiving her differently. She went to the kitchen. I heard the refrigerator door open and close. Then she returned with a glass of water in her hand. "Here," she said.

I took a big gulp of water. It helped. Most of the images, information and material that had been fed to me while I was out of my body were gone. Still, some remained. I shook my head again. "Jeez, I feel like I've been tripping."

"In a sense, maybe you were," Rusty said. "What happened?"

"I saw an angel," I finally said, feeling rather stupid now that I had said it.

"An angel?" both Rusty and Dave exclaimed together.

"Yeah, an angel," I continued. "Only, not just any angel. The Angel of Sound. Named Shamael."

"You talked to it?" Rusty asked.

"That and more," I said. "I can't really tell you about it now. It's a bit too much for me to handle. But this angel, Shamael, he wants me to somehow oversee how the Lost Chord is used."

"What?" both Rusty and Dave exclaimed together.

"Yeah, and there's a lot more. I saw past and future lives, got all sorts of cosmic information about things—no, not just information—experiences. I had all these different experiences and understandings. Most of it's faded by now. I still have glimpses of some of what happened, though I can't talk about it now. But I particularly remember the angel, and what it wanted from me."

"You really saw an angel?" Rusty said again. She was impressed. I was trying to process.

"Rusty," I began, "This Lost Chord is much bigger than I ever imagined. Maybe bigger than anything you've ever imagined. It creates a kind of interdimensional gateway that allows whoever is listening to the Chord to travel to the dimensionality that is best suited for them."

Rusty nodded her head. "That may be right," she said. "I had an extraordinary experience of being on a starship, talking with extraterrestrial beings."

"You never told me that," Dave said.

"I didn't want to influence your experience," Rusty answered.

"But I only traveled through the solar system," Dave said in a saddened tone. "I didn't meet any extraterrestrials or meet any angels."

I looked at Dave and smiled with compassion. "Comparing experiences like this doesn't serve any purpose—especially if you're going to be envious of someone else's experiences. We all went to places which were best suited for us." I turned to Rusty, "Did these extraterrestrials that you spoke with say anything about the Lost Chord. Had they helped influence you in creating it? Maybe assisted you, either consciously or unconsciously, with the technology to build it?"

Rusty nodded her head. "I think they did. How did you know that?"

"Just a lucky guess," I said. But it wasn't really. On one level, Rusty had stumbled across the frequencies to create the Lost Chord. On another dimension, however, I understood that she had received help. It made sense and it seemed to indicate that some type of beings were interested in having the Lost Chord manifest on the physical plane. Whether their intentions were positive or negative, I wasn't sure.

I sat back trying to take in all that I had experienced.

"Shade," Rusty began. "You look different. Calmer and more relaxed than I think I've ever seen you."

"No," I said with a smile. "I think I'm nearly stunned. That's what happens when an archangel blasts open your third eye."

"You're kidding," Rusty exclaimed, shrieking with delight. "That's incredible."

Dave was looking glum. "I wish I had had my third eye opened by an angel."

"Don't worry," I said. "I'm sure you will. But there's something more important going on right now."

"What do you mean?" Rusty asked.

I tried to sit up as straight as I could. "Rusty," I

began, "How many people have you played the Lost Chord for?"

"Just you and David, thus far. I only just completed it late last night. But I can get lots of other people to hear it. In fact, I've got Jay Lawson coming over in a few hours," she said, looking at her watch.

Dave looked at his watch. "Shade, man. We've got to go. The gig's going to be happening in a half hour."

I dismissed his statement with a wave of my hand and addressed my words to Rusty. "No, Rusty, you don't understand. I don't want you to interest more people."

"Who do you think you are?" Rusty asked haughtily.

"That came out wrong," I said. "The angel I spoke with warned me about the dangers of using the Lost Chord. The dangers of it falling into the wrong hands and being misused."

"Don't worry, Shade," Rusty said. "I won't let anybody do anything with the Lost Chord. I just want to try it with a few other people. Do you know how long I've been working on this project?"

"Yes, I know Rusty. But how well do you know Jay Lawson?" I asked. Lawson was another musician and scientist. Boulder was full of them.

"Better than I know you," she said.

"Please, Rusty," I pleaded. "You really have no idea how powerful the Lost Chord is. It's addictive."

"Oh, Shade," Rusty sighed.

"How many times have you tried it since you found it last night?" I asked.

"Well, I did make myself a little thirty second disk that I have tried several times," she admitted. "However, it didn't effect me in the same manner as a complete five minute exposure to the frequencies. A short burst of it seemed to only induce an altered state for about fifteen minutes. Nothing spectacular happened. It didn't really put me aboard the starship like my first experience."

"You tried it three times in the last day, after your initial experience?" I said. "I rest my case."

"Shade, you're being ridiculous," she laughed.

"I can afford to be ridiculous," I defended. "I've just had a conversation with an angel. And I'm definitely considering myself a messenger from God. How much more ridiculous can you get?"

"Look, Shade," she said. "I know you've had a tremendous experience. I'm sure it was truly transformational. However, you can't start dictating the actions of others. That's one of the primary spiritual laws."

"How do you know?" I asked. I checked the primary spiritual laws which were now floating around somewhere in my consciousness. "You're right," I said, nodding my head. "I can't make you do something, but I can advise you on various topics. And I am advising you not to let anyone else listen to, or even know about the Lost Chord until we've had a serious conversation."

"We are having a serious conversation," she said.

"Listen Rusty, I need time to process the experience I just had. Things are swimming around in my head that you wouldn't believe. And I think my psychic abilities have been enhanced, because I can feel Dave being impatient and waiting to take me to the gig."

"I am!" Dave affirmed.

"That's not being psychic," Rusty laughed. "David's pacing around here, acting nervous as a mother cat about to have kittens."

"No, seriously," I told her. "I've gone through some really deep changes in myself—in my consciousness and understanding. I sense things and know things that I've never felt or experienced before. But I've really got to leave now. I can't do much more than try to persuade you not to do anything with the Lost Chord right now. The gig at the Dugout is over at one. We can come by then to discuss things. I know there's something more important that I need to tell you, but right now I just can't think straight."

"Go play some guitar," Rusty said confidently. "I'm sure it'll do you some good."

"Call Lawson now and tell him not to come over," I said. "Please. I have a bad feeling about this."

Dave took my hand and pulled me up. "Come on Shade, we've got to go."

"Please, Rusty. I have a bad feeling about this. Promise me you won't let Lawson know about the Lost Chord. And whatever you do, don't let him listen to it." Dave was now pulling me to the door.

"He already knows about it," Rusty said. "And I can't promise you anything. I will think about what you've said and I will do what I think is proper. After all, it is my discovery."

Dave had me out the door and walking towards his car. "Please!" I shouted back at Rusty.

"I'll think about it," she said before closing the door.

"Damn!" I said.

We were now at Dave's car. "What's the matter?" he asked as he opened the door.

"I know there was something else I should have said. I know I could have handled it differently," I said.

"Don't worry, Shade," Dave said. "I think you're doing pretty good for a fellow who just wrestled with an angel." Then he started the car and we were off to the Dugout. How was I going to play?

CHAPTER 7

It was a Tuesday night, and therefore not a particularly high volume night at the Dugout, despite the Ladies 2 for 1 drink special. Sometimes the 2 for 1 brought in the college kids. Other times, it didn't. Tonight was one of them. I think the weather may have had something to do with it. It was February, and while it wasn't snowing, it was cold—somewhere in the 30's. Most people were staying in. I kind of wished I was one of them.

Despite the fact that Dave had missed sound check, we had no problems with the sound. We had been playing together long enough so that if we wanted to see how the mix sounded, I'd go in front of the band while everyone else played, check the sound and then reset the levels, if necessary. Actually, this is what we often did, which is why it was no big deal that Dave had missed sound check. It was the principle of the thing. If everyone got into missing sound check, then we'd have a problem. So, we always made it to sound check, or usually we did.

We played three sets that night and it was nothing to be proud of. I wasn't the only one who was off. For the other band members, it probably had to do with the weather and lack of people. For me it had to do with the fact that I had barely recovered from having the most profound experience of my life. And while I was able to hit the right notes and sing the right words, there wasn't a hell of a lot of feeling either. It was like blues by rote. I don't think those few people who were in the club really minded. We didn't sound bad, just bland. There was no fire in the songs. Even "Hootchie Koochie Man" and "Red House" were lacking.

I couldn't get over the image of that 9 foot angel giving me an assignment to watch over the Lost Chord, nor the blur of visions, images, information, knowledge and experiences that I had been privy to. As I said, certain things seemed to remain. And I did seem to have some sort of enhancement of my psychic powers (which was not very hard to do, because before the Lost Chord experience, I think I had virtually none). Sometimes when I wasn't thinking about the angel, I'd look around the bar and see if I could get thoughts or flashes from the people in the bar. It was fascinating. But you can understand why my playing was less than dynamic. I had other things on my mind.

The night dragged by slowly. When I heard the signal for last call, I breathed a sigh of relief. I couldn't help thinking about Rusty and Jay Lawson. I didn't know Lawson. I knew of him. He was a local musician; a jazz player, but I knew he also delved into the esoteric. I thought, as a matter of fact, he was a devotee of Uncle Jude, who has modulated between being a national musician and a local guru. Jude's got a place outside of Gold Hill. Lawson was one of his right hand men. The more I thought about Lawson showing up at Rusty's, the less I liked it. I didn't know if it was my newly opened third eye, or just extreme paranoia. I was, however, really anxious to get back to Rusty's as soon as possible.

When the last number of the last set was completed, I unplugged my guitar, a '62 Fender Stratocaster, put it into my case, closed it, and waved good-by to everyone.

"What's the rush?" Bill Nickels, our competent bass player asked.

"Ask Dave," I said, heading out the door. "He knows where I'm going."

"Do you want me to go with you, Shade?" Dave called from behind his synthesizer.

"Nah, just meet me there," I yelled back. I had parked my vehicle behind the Dugout before sound check. It was an '88 Ford Bronco II, not very big on looks but very effective in the snow. It was blue and white, colors that appealed to me at the time I bought it from a used car dealership. I laid my Strat carefully down in the back, covered it with a blanket I kept there and then attempted to start my car. It took three tries, but the engine finally caught. I let the vehicle warm up for a couple of minutes, then put it into first and took off. I still could not shake this nasty feeling I had as I drove the short distance to Rusty's.

I knocked twice before she answered the door. She looked terrible. Her eyes were red. I knew she had been crying.

I walked in, closing the door and cold air behind me. "Rusty, what happened?"

"I can't believe it, Shade!" she said bitterly.

"What can't you believe, Rusty?" I asked, as gently as I could. I did not like the sound of this at all.

"I can't believe it, Shade. You were right."

This sounded worse than I had imagined. "What was I right about, Rusty?" I asked, but I knew before she said anything.

"Lawson has the program. He's got the Lost Chord.

He stole the disk. We've got to get it back!" Her tone was laced with anger.

"What happened?" I asked.

"He came over a few hours ago as we had arranged. Truthfully, Shade, your words of warning stayed with me. They affected me more than I knew. I wasn't even going to let Jay listen to the Lost Chord. But he's so smooth and suave—a real charmer. I let him experience the Chord. He loved it and had his own vision of nirvana. He was so excited. He asked if he could have a copy of the program to take to Uncle Jude, that Anti-Christ up in the mountains. I told him absolutely not. He said 'okay' and was gone shortly after that. Sometime between the time he re-entered his body and the time he went out the door, he took the Lost Chord disk program. I don't know how, but I haven't been thinking clearly. It's been such a long day."

"Is that the only copy?" I asked?

"No, of course not. I have a backup. But it means that we've already lost control. Less than six hours after you warned me to take care, I loose the Lost Chord. Damn!" she said bitterly. Suddenly, she was crying again. Just as suddenly, I had her in my arms, comforting her. It was amazing. Despite all my sexual attraction to this woman, there was absolutely nothing sexual about this experience. Granted, there was a lot of energy coming from my heart, but nothing from my root chakra. I was truly amazed. Maybe I was a changed man?

"It's okay," I said softly, stroking her hair. "We'll get it back."

"No, we can't," she sobbed. "It's gone."

"Where does he live?" I asked. "I'll go over and get it back. I promise I will."

"He's not at his house," she said. She looked at me and sighed. "If you're so psychic, tell me. Where is Jay Lawson?"

The words immediately popped in my head without thinking, although, I would have figured it out myself if I hadn't been so tired. "Uncle Jude's," I said.

"Uncle Jude's," she repeated, nodding her head.

Just then, there was a knock on the door. It was Dave. In about a minute, we were able to tell him about the situation.

"Oh man, I can't believe it," Dave said. "Should we call the police?"

"What?" I laughed. "And report a stolen computer disk?"

"But it's like industrial espionage," Dave said.

"We need James Bond," I replied a bit more seriously. "Luckily, you've got Christopher Shade, Spiritual Detective, on hand." That got a smile out of Rusty who had stopped crying, but was sitting around with a long face while I talked.

"What do you know about Uncle Jude?" I asked. "I've never met him, but I've heard some interesting stories. I think he has some sort of community up in the mountains around Gold Hill."

"Well," Dave began, "He was a kind of a national success in the late 60's and early 70's with his group Uncle Jude's Band. They had the hit, 'Magical Man', which I think went platinum, and a follow up that I can't remember, but also did pretty well."

"It was called 'Enchanted Love', I believe," I called out. I have always been good at song titles.

"That's right," Dave said. "Every so often, he'll get a

group of people together and go on revival tours. Mostly, he has a commune going on in the mountains. Actually, I think it's more of a cult and he's the leader. I've never been there, but I've heard that he's worshiped as some sort of messiah."

"He's the closest thing I've ever seen to the Anti-Christ!" Rusty added angrily.

"How do you know?" I asked, rather astounded that she actually knew Uncle Jude.

"I lived there for a short time when I first came to Boulder. I was searching for something then—peace of mind, God—I don't know what. His followers convinced me that Uncle Jude was a fully enlightened and self-realized being. They invited me up to his commune to experience the bliss he could initiate."

It struck me as amusing that a rock n' roll musician would become some sort of self-proclaimed messiah. I did have to acknowledge that perhaps this was what many performers on stage were looking for—adulation and love. Most musicians were trying to receive this love from an audience's applause. Uncle Jude had found an easier method—become the voice of God and receive this love from his followers. The absurdity of it was difficult for me to imagine, although I could appreciate the cleverness of the situation. I had heard about Uncle Jude before. I had simply never believed the stories. They seemed ridiculous to me.

"He's really got followers?" I asked.

"He certainly does," Rusty answered. "When I was there, there were about twenty or thirty people who lived with him all the time. They followed his every word as gospel and would do anything he asked. I spent a few days there before I left." She was silent for a few moments.

"And?" I asked.

"He's quite a powerful man and a monstrously controlling individual," she finally answered. "He's worshiped as though he's a living god at the commune. It's really terrifying. That's why I had to leave. Yet, at the same time, he does have quite an understanding of sound. In fact, it was because of him that I became interested in trying to find the Lost Chord."

"Whew!" I breathed. "No wonder Lawson was so interested in getting that disk to him." I shook my head wearily. "Well, it's gone full circle now hasn't it." I looked at Rusty. "But why did you call him the Anti-Christ." I was seeing pictures now, getting visions. But I really didn't know if they were coming from me or from her.

"Christopher, the man is the most spiritually corrupt being I have ever met. All he's interested in is power. He is also the most self-serving human I've ever encountered. He's charismatic and despite an additional twenty or thirty pounds that he's put on since his glory days, is still quite beautiful looking. He loves to manipulate and control."

It was only the second time since I'd known Rusty that she'd called me Christopher. I liked it. I did not, however, like the situation that seemed to have evolved. "Sounds like your typical cult messianic figure," I said, trying to lighten the atmosphere which was so thick you could almost slice it.

"I'm serious, Shade," Rusty said, wiping her face with her hand. "The man is ruthless. He wanted to have sex with me when I first arrived at his commune. I was charmed by him, but still quite young and shy. I told him no. Using his guards to assist him, the bastard raped me. He told me it was for my own good—that it would raise my vibrations and bring me closer to God. That's why I left the commune."

"Why didn't you report him?" I asked angrily.

"He laughed when I threatened to do that. He told me he had witnesses there who saw me giving myself to him out of my own free will. He told me that if I ever bothered him in any way, he'd see to it that I was killed." She looked at me. I continued to see the images. They were real. "I knew he was serious," Rusty continued. "That was the last I saw of him. It was years ago, but obviously he's still around. And now he's gained control of the Lost Chord!"

"This is bad," Dave said. "Real bad."

"It could get worse," I said.

"How?" Dave asked.

"We could try to get the Chord back from him," I replied. Both Dave and Rusty looked at me with puzzlement. "Only joking," I assured them.

"What do we do?" Rusty asked.

"We've got to come up with a plan," Dave said. "We can't just go up there and demand he give the Lost Chord back to us."

"Why not?" I asked. "Let's give the man a chance. Maybe he's changed after all these years, Rusty".

"Sure," Rusty said sarcastically. "And maybe I'm the Dalai Lama".

"Hello, Dolly!" I joked. Neither of them laughed. Then I added: "First thing tomorrow morning let's go up together and talk to Uncle Jude at his community. We'll go up there with no agenda and just speak to the man. Maybe we're being paranoid for nothing."

"No, we should go up and demand it from him now,"

Rusty said fiercely. "Before he's had any real time to do anything with the Lost Chord."

"Rusty, if we show up in the middle of the night, I'd say that the man might be a bit on the defensive. In fact, we'd probably get shot." I took a step towards the door. "Listen. I'm going home and getting some sleep. After that experience today and everything else that has happened, I'm beat."

"You could sleep here," Rusty said. She looked at Dave. "You both could. I've got a spare bedroom."

"Many thanks," I said, heading out the door. "I'll be much better off in the morning. Meet you both here at nine o'clock sharp."

Then, I was off. Pictures were flashing through my mind. Beings were speaking to me. Heaven and Hell were battling it out in my consciousness. I needed sleep.

The ride back to my house took maybe ten minutes. It was about all I could do to stay awake. I was so beat, I left my guitar in the back of the Bronco. I knew it would be okay. Once I got into my apartment, I turned off the phone, set the alarm for 8 am, and then lay down on my bed. I was asleep before my head hit the pillow.

CHAPTER 8

I slept soundly that night. If I dreamed, I didn't remember it. It had been an exhausting day, and my body and brain refreshed themselves in the deep sea of Morpheus.

I woke up at 8 o'clock the next day, thanks to the help of my alarm. I felt refreshed and exhilarated. Some of my out of body experiences of the day before remained with me, especially my tete a tete with the angel. Thankfully, it seemed like most of my other visions and sounds had faded. There was still a fleeting image of a past lifetime or two, but the really heavy memories and experiences were gone. Or suppressed. Either was alright with me.

I sat down with a cup of coffee and tried to assess the day's activities. While my non-physical realities had softened, the actual be here now material had hardened in my mind. We had to go see Uncle Jude. This was nothing I was looking forward to.

I am mostly a private type of person. I like to perform, and on occasion, party around with others. But I also like my private time. I could have really used it this morning. I am mostly a gentle person, too. If tested and pushed against the wall, I will push back. However, I am not really an aggressive type, except perhaps with women, and I think we're talking about a different type of aggression here. In truth, as I sat there nursing my morning cup of coffee, I realized that the last thing I wanted to do was face Uncle Jude.

Perhaps it was just that I was scared. That would have been reason enough. But it was more than that. There was something about facing an ancient enemy that was being whispered in the back of my head by a voice that I didn't want to hear. This concept of "ancient enemy" implied many things that were worse then going one on one with a psychotic cult leader. It implied, as did my past lifetime visions, that I had been here before. That was a belief system I didn't want to encounter this early in the morning.

I looked outside. It was a bright, sunny Boulder day and I figured the weather had changed at last. It would probably go on up to the 50's or 60's if we were lucky. Still, when I dressed, I prepared for the weather up in the mountains, which could be a good 10 to 20 degrees colder. I put on a tee-shirt and jeans, then layered my dressing with a sweater. When I left at 8:45, after a shave and a shower, I had also put on my winter jacket with gloves in the pocket.

I arrived at Rusty's place about 9 am. Dave's car was pulling up just as I rang Rusty's front door buzzer. She opened it up immediately. She looked terrible.

"You look terrible," I said. "Didn't you get any sleep?"

"Not much," she said. "Where's David?"

I motioned behind me to the figure coming up the walk. I waved to him. He waved back. Then I walked into the condo. Rusty stayed at the door until Dave came in, shutting the door behind them both.

"Sleep okay, Dave?" I asked, pulling off my coat and

collapsing on the couch.

"Fine, Shade. And you?"

"Most excellently," I assured him. I pointed to Rusty. "It does not, however, look like our red headed friend here has had too much rest."

"Shut up Shade!" she said. "Do either of you want any coffee?"

"We really should be off," I said. "The early bird catches the worm and all that other jazz."

"Have you come up with any plan?" Dave asked me.

"No," I said, shaking my head. I guess as lead guitarist of the Cosmic Blues Band, I was the unofficial leader. In a way, I suppose that role permeated the rest of my life. It wasn't necessarily true, but then again, it seemed I had no choice. It was obvious Dave Baer hadn't been racking his rather significant brains deciding what to do. Still I thought I'd ask. "Have you?"

"No," he answered, scratching his beard.

"How about you, Rusty?" I asked.

She shook her head sadly, not saying anything.

"Okay," I began. "I think maybe that what I came up with last night—just driving up to see Uncle Jude and talking straight with him might be the best plan. At least it's a start."

"I don't like it," Rusty interjected. "He's ruthless and cunning and more manipulative than you can believe. I don't see what we can accomplish by openly confronting him."

"Do you have any better plan?" I asked.

Rusty ran a hand through her long red hair. "No," she replied sadly, "I guess I don't, Shade."

I wondered what happened to her references to me being "Christopher", as she had called me the night before. I decided not to say anything about it. Instead, I continued to focus on the problem immediately at hand. "Well then, let's go for it. And let's not assume the worst." I looked at Rusty. Then at Dave. "Did either of you try to call Lawson this morning?"

"I did," Rusty said. "I just got his answering machine. He's probably at Uncle Jude's Ranch right now."

"The Ranch?" I asked.

"His compound up in the mountains," Rusty replied.

"Oh," I answered, nodding my head. "Then I suggest we head up there ourselves." I began to walk towards the door. I turned to see the other two following me.

Once we were in the Bronco driving up Boulder Canyon for the mountains, I asked two pertinent questions. The first was: "Does anyone know how to get there?" I had assumed that Rusty did, that is, if she could still remember.

"The Ranch is on a dirt road off 72, outside Nederland, near Gold Hill," she told me.

"Left or right?" I asked.

"A left," she replied. "Then about a half mile later another left. We won't miss the Ranch. It's surrounded by an eight foot electrified fence. You'll see it amidst all the trees, I can assure you."

"You're kidding," I said, but I knew she wasn't. Uncle Jude Primer was a legendary figure in this part of the country. Part messiah, part monster, and part myth I was sure. Every year or so one of the local papers would run an article on the man and his community. Supposedly in the early 70's after a number of his newer releases had flopped, he had had a vision, letting him know that the world as we knew it was going to end and that a new regime was about to occur. Uncle Jude had begun gathering followers at his ranch to help him bring in this new era. I had been totally cynical about his vision until now. Having had an experience as I had the day before made me less skeptical about such things. However, I did know that the Ranch had been in operation for about 30 years, and thus far Armageddon had not happened yet. Still, I knew from my brief experience of the day before that time and space are not everything that they appear to be. Perhaps from a more cosmic viewpoint, 30 years is just a wink in the eye of an angel (I could not remember if Shamael had blinked or not, but the concept seemed appropriate). Perhaps Uncle Jude was growing tired of waiting for the end. Perhaps he wanted to use the Lost Chord to help usher it in. I didn't know.

My second question to Rusty was more specific than the one for directions, and I knew it would require a more lengthy explanation. I thought this was probably okay, because as we drove up the mountain she seemed pretty depressed. I guess I would have been, too, if I had been her.

"How does the Lost Chord work, Rusty?" I asked as we passed through Nederland and drove on 72 towards Gold Hill.

"I wish I knew, Shade," she said. "I wish I knew."

"What?" I exclaimed.

"I was trying to combine a lot of different psycho-acoustic effects," she began. I knew she'd have more to say than, "I wish I knew." I was right. She continued talking about the Chord. "I've been experimenting with the effects of different frequencies and their combined harmonics for a long time. I've been working alone, experimenting on myself. First, I tried working with beat frequencies."

Beat frequencies, as I have explained, are the phenomenon that occur when two very closely related sounds are created together. They create a third sound, the result of the two primary sounds beating against each other, which has the potential of changing brain wave activity. While this sound can be played through speakers in a room and played at inaudible levels, it is not that effective. It certainly was not the Lost Chord.

"Then I started working with Pythagorean intervals," Rusty continued. "I worked mainly with the perfect fifth, which seemed to be most effective. I added that interval to the beat frequencies and it made it more powerful."

An interval is the difference between two notes. In today's music, particularly music that is played on keyboards, the relationship of notes, such as C and a G, has been changed from how it would normally occur in nature. In nature, there are frequencies, called harmonics or overtones, which are created whenever a string is plucked or air passes through a tube. They are naturally occurring sounds, which are geometrically related. They are very powerful. Harmonics create the interval that Rusty was talking about. The harmonically related interval of the fifth has two notes sounding together which vibrate at a ratio of 3:2. It has the ability of putting the brain into very deep states. Like the beat frequency phenomenon, it also has the ability to synchronize the left and right hemispheres of the brain which increases the ability to induce altered states of consciousness. This was knowledge that the ancient civilizations such as the Egyptians and the Greeks were aware of. We'd just forgotten it. Still, it wasn't the Lost Chord.

"Then I began working with specific frequencies to stimulate particular areas of the brain like the pineal and pituitary," Rusty said, nodding her head up and down as though talking to herself. "This is where it became a little scary. I found some information on research scientists who claimed they had discovered the frequencies of the pituitary and pineal gland. Then, I tried them. They made the sounds that I was working with even more effective. Then, I remember reading that one of the scientists had died of a brain hemorrhage and I wondered if the two were related."

I would have wondered, too. The pineal and pituitary are part of the endocrine system, the ductless gland systems. These two glands are in the brain. The pituitary is called "the master gland" and it seems to be involved with growth, as well as with controlling the other glands. This is what is scientifically acknowledged. The pineal is an organ that Descartes thought was the "seat of the soul". It has something to do with our relationship to light, and used to be known as the third eye. It also seems to control the pituitary. Esoterically, these two glands are associated with those energy centers which I told you about, called chakras. The pineal and pituitary glands were related to the top two head chakras—the third eye and the crown. Similar to my experience with having my third eye opened by Shamael, Rusty had been experimenting doing the same thing with sound.

"Anything else?" I asked. I could see that Rusty had really been investigating the cutting edge technologies of sound. It was fascinating. And frightening as well. Still, I knew that despite all those frequencies she had mentioned, she could not have created the Lost Chord. There had to be something else.

Rusty was sitting in the front seat next to me. She turned and looked at me. "If that had been all, everything would have been okay. But I kept going. I knew there was more that could be done. I started programming mantras into my computer. I had figured out a way of taking the sacred words and turning them into frequencies."

"What!" I exclaimed. I knew that this was the missing ingredient. Mantras were sacred words of power from different traditions. They were usually chanted aloud, although they were sometimes whispered or even intoned silently. No one had ever figured out how to turn mantras into frequencies.

"Don't ask me how I did this," Rusty said, getting excited about her work and forgetting about the potential trouble it could cause. "It was just a lucky guess. I made the assumption that mantras were really sonic formulas for specific wave forms. In other words, the 'Om' not only was a mantra, a sacred word, but also it had a specific frequency. It was, in fact, a very specific composite of different frequencies."

Rusty nodded to herself. "You know, the 'Om' makes a shape as well," she said. "Actually, almost any sound can creates a shape, but the 'Om' creates a very special shape. Years ago, a scientist discovered that if he put different substances like sand, liquids, and plastics, on a plate and then vibrated these plates with sound, the different substances took on incredibly organic and geometric looking forms. He used mostly pure tones, but sometime later, someone else used the voice to create shapes. They had someone chant 'Om' and then put that sound into one of those plates with sand in it. The 'Om' sound created this shape that looked like a big circle with many little triangles inside intersecting each other. It's the same shape that the ancient mystics thousands of years ago pictured as being a visual representation of the 'Om'. It's called the Shri Yantra and is a mandala found in tens of thousands of Hindu temples. People use this image to meditate and enter altered states. It's especially powerful when you chant 'Om' and look at it. Isn't that incredible?"

"Yeah, sure," I mumbled, not really understanding.

"Well," Rusty continued, "Once I understood about the 'Om', that it was really a composite frequency, I began to put all these sacred chants into the Lost Chord. You understand, of course, they were no longer vocal chants. They had become tones. They were frequencies."

"No, I don't understand," I admitted.

"It's really hard to explain. I'm not even sure I understand myself. I began with the vowel sounds. I understood that the different vowel sounds had different harmonics. Every vowel sound has its own particular harmonics that are specific to it. This was not all that difficult to program into the computer since harmonics are geometrically related and just pure math."

"I guess," I said, still not following.

"Then I programmed in the consonant sounds. This was where I really took a guess. It was a shot in the dark so to speak. Who could come up with a coherent numerical value for a consonant? It's all speculation. There are lots of different systems that people have created assigning numerical values to consonants. Lots of different systems and values, but no one agrees. I knew that I had to start somewhere. So, I did, and it worked."

"What did you use as the frequencies for the consonants?" I asked, trying to comprehend.

"I didn't know where to start. There were an infinite

amount of possible numbers that could be used. So, I just played around. For the sound of the 'm', which of course is in the 'Om' sound," she laughed, "I programmed in my birth date."

"Your what?" I couldn't believe my ears.

"My birth date! I used my birthdate for the frequency of the 'm' in the 'Om' and it worked!" She giggled. "It was the missing piece of the Lost Chord. Once I had decoded the frequencies of the 'Om', I was able to figure out all the other consonants, and then feed the sacred names of God and sacred chants from other traditions into the computer."

Shamael had been right. The discovery of the Lost Chord had been totally accidental. At least from our point of understanding. I knew that there had undoubtedly been forces which had been working through Rusty to help her. I could not at the time figure out whether these forces were good or bad or both.

"Let me get this straight," I said. "You figured out how to turn mantras and other sacred names and words into sounds."

"Yes," she said. "I programmed in mantras and God names from all the different traditions, including Tibetan, Hebrew, Sanskrit, and Arabic. There's even ancient Egyptian and Sumarian. There are over 3,300 different frequencies in the Lost Chord. And that's just from the mantras and God names I used."

"It sounds like you're talking about white noise," I said. White noise, like white light, was a composite of all different frequencies. Many nature sounds, such as the ocean, are composite frequencies that are heard as white noise.

"Yes," Rusty admitted. "But these sounds create a very specific white noise when used in combination with all those other frequencies that I've told you about. Do you remember what the Lost Chord had sounded like?"

It was the first time I'd thought about it. There wasn't much to remember. "No," I said honestly. "I remember that it sounded something like the wind and the water and there were some sounds that made me think of outer space. You know, I can't remember anything really specific."

"Well," she began. "It's not really a chord in the way that we normally think of chords. It's really a combination of frequencies and harmonically related tones that do seem like white noise. When you hear it, on an acoustic level, the Lost Chord doesn't sound as though it were created on an instrument. It's not like trumpets blaring or anything orchestral. It's very subtle. Yet, it is a chord, since chords are really just composite frequencies."

"And it creates interdimensional gateways," I said a bit sadly. "You really did it right, Rusty," I shook my head. "Or wrong. But it's here now."

We had been driving along Highway 72 while Rusty and I talked. Magnificent snow capped mountains had been in our view almost the entire time. Sometimes 72 was icy, and when that happened I would drive with my heart racing. A skid on this highway could mean a drop off the road for hundreds or thousands of feet. We were 9,000 feet up in the mountains and it was a cautious traveler who drove this highway. Despite our recent snow, the highway was pretty clean and the trip was not nearly as terrifying as it had been at other times. I usually did not like to go on 72 in the winter if at all possible. Today I wasn't scared. Maybe it was because Rusty's talking was taking my attention away from driving off the road and rolling over. Or maybe it was because I was aware of a much more real and present danger other than an icy road.

As she talked, I drove. Then she said, "Turn left there!" I did. We were on a dirt road that was well maintained. There was about an inch of snow, but it was nothing my Bronco couldn't handle. We drove for about half a mile. Then Rusty said, "There!", again, and I took another left. Mostly we had been seeing trees and snow. Then all of a sudden there was a hideous metal fence and a big "Private Property" and "Keep Out" sign.

Rusty had been right. I wouldn't have been able to miss it if I'd tried.

CHAPTER 9

A compound is a compound is a compound, I thought. And a cult is a cult is a cult. There was no doubt about it. We were not in Kansas anymore. The eight foot steel electric fence was a foreboding sign—let alone the actual posted messages. There was an ominous feeling in the air as I stopped the car to survey the area. I was not sure if it was due to my enhanced psychic ability, or just the obvious sensations you would feel when approaching a place like Auschwitz, where terrible things had happened or were about to happen.

"There's an entrance over there," Dave called from the backseat. As he said it, I saw that there was an opening in the electrified fence; a gate was swung open, with a plowed dirt road leading back into the compound area. There were no guards.

"Shall we?" I asked. No one said anything. I guided the Bronco through the gate and headed down the road.

"This is trespassing, I think," Dave said glumly. "We could get shot."

"Nonsense, Dave my friend," I replied in a glib and light hearted manner. The atmosphere was so thick you could cut it with a knife. "We are here merely to visit the master of the house. A cordial visit is all."

"Right," Dave said. Rusty said nothing. I patted her

gently on her thigh and smiled.

"It'll be all right," I said. "Honest."

There were acres of beautiful snow laden pines that we passed as we drove down the private road. Then, ahead, I saw it. It loomed in the distance like a dark behemoth.

"Is that it?" I asked.

Rusty nodded. All she said was: "The Ranch."

The Ranch was indeed a ranch style structure. It was huge. Three stories high. Made of wood. It looked like a giant log cabin that sprawled over the landscape as we approached. It could have been a hotel or hospitality house. Maybe that's how it began. But there was something very uninviting about the place. I couldn't put my finger or my third eye on it. It looked normal and yet there was a cold and clammy energy that I felt. There were windows in the building. All of them had shades or shutters and I couldn't see in.

The dirt road ended in a circular driveway at the entrance to the ranch. There were steps leading to an entrance on the second story of the building. I looked at Dave and then at Rusty.

"Shall we go in?" I asked, "Say hello to our Uncle Jude?"

"I don't think that's necessary," Dave said, his voice full of fear, as he pointed over my shoulder.

Two men were approaching us, coming down the steps that led to the entrance to the ranch. They were both dressed normally, in blue jeans and flannel shirts. I had expected maybe men in turbans and togas.

Both men had beards. Both men were big, muscular and kind of beefy. They both must have been at least six and a half feet tall, and probably weighed at least 300 pounds apiece. They could have passed as loggers or miners in this mountainous area, or bears for that matter.

One man came over to the driver's side. The other went over to Rusty's side. She sank down in her seat. I pulled down my window.

"Howdy," I said, affecting my best congenial mountain dialect.

"Can we help you?" the guard standing outside my car door said to me.

"Yes," I replied, smiling my best toothy smile. "We're here to see Uncle Jude."

"Do you have an appointment?" this guard asked.

"An appointment?" I repeated. "No, we don't. But one of us is an old friend of Jude's. He'll be anxious to see us."

"I don't think so," said my guard. "He's very busy."

Suddenly, I looked annoyed. I turned to Rusty and Dave shaking my head. "See, we should have called from Boulder. But no, you wanted it to be a surprise."

Rusty and Dave's mouths dropped open. I immediately brought this guard's attention back to me by speaking: "Okay," I said to him. "If you don't want to bother him, I can understand. But, I will call as soon as I find a phone and tell him that we were up to visit, and that you wouldn't let us in."

"You know Uncle Jude?" my guard asked.

"Some of us know him intimately," I replied. At that moment, I felt like Obi-Wan Kenobi in *Star Wars*. "Call him. Get him for us," was all I said. The guard at my side nodded his head.

"Who should I tell him is calling?" he asked.

"It's a surprise. We're old friends. Get him for us." I said calmly, yet assuredly.

The guard I had been speaking with nodded his head. Then he turned and headed up the front steps. "Come on, Butch," he said, motioning to the other guard. This guard looked puzzled for a second. Then he turned and followed.

We waited in the Bronco, motor running, heater on, for about five minutes before the front door to the Ranch opened again. There was Uncle Jude heading down the stairs, being followed by the two guards.

I had seen various pictures of Jude Primer, but he had looked different in all of them. Sometimes he appeared almost angelic—clean shaven with long blonde hair. Sometimes his visage had seemed positively demonic—a dark beard and darker hair. Sometimes he was slender. Sometimes he was fat. He was like a chameleon, I guess.

This time he was more on the pudgy side than not. And he was clean shaven, back to dying his shoulder length hair blond. He wasn't dressed in robes or anything either, which was a bit disappointing for me. I had seen him in that spiritual looking garb, but I suppose that was just for ceremonial occasions. He was wearing jeans and a dirty white sweatshirt. I didn't see anything special about him yet. He looked tired and spacey, as if he had been up all night, which I no doubt assumed was true.

Uncle Jude looked annoyed as he walked toward my Bronco, followed by the two guards. I turned off the car engine as he approached my side of the vehicle. He gazed at me hard, obviously scanning his memory banks for some recollection of me.

"Do I know you?" he asked harshly.

I smiled. "Hello, Jude," I said. "It's good to see you." I pointed to Rusty. "You remember Rusty Fox don't you?"

Uncle Jude cast a fleeting glance at Rusty. Then back to me. "No," he said. "And I don't remember you either."

"Well it's been a while," I began. "In fact, it's been ten years since you and Rusty last encountered each other." Then I looked him directly in his baby blue eyes. "And we sir, have never met."

"What is this?" Uncle Jude asked, "A joke? What's this about?" His face was beginning to turn into a snarl. I could see he could become ugly very quickly.

I tried to remain calm and focused. "This is about something very important. It is about the Lost Chord."

"Lost Chord?" he repeated. "I don't know what you're talking about."

"Yes, you do, Jude," I affirmed. "It was brought to you last night by Jay Lawson. You do know Jay Lawson don't you?"

"Lawson?" Uncle Jude repeated. "Yes, I know Lawson. He's one of my finest students."

Students. I liked that. I thought he would have said "Disciples," or something like that. I continued looking him in the eye. "Well, Lawson took something from this lady," I said pointing again at Rusty. "Something that I know he brought to you. Something that's very important."

"What are you talking about?" Uncle Jude asked, his irritation growing.

"A computer disk," I told him, point blank. "With a series of frequencies on it that induces altered states of consciousness." I paused for a moment. "I know you know what I'm talking about. I can look at you and see that you've just come from having experienced it."

Primer's eyes widened. He said nothing. I think he was accessing me.

"I know you've got these frequencies," I stated firmly. "What we call the Lost Chord. We've got to talk about it."

"Why?" Primer said, coldly. "What's it to you if I do?"

I shook my head sadly. "There are many different reasons for talking to you about it. But most importantly, I've got to tell you that there are things about those frequencies that you don't know."

"What are you talking about?" Primer said in disgust. I was sure that he was still dazed by his experience with the Lost Chord.

"There are things about the Lost Chord that you don't know," I repeated. "Things we have to tell you. Things that Lawson doesn't know about. Things that are dangerous, maybe even deadly, about the Lost Chord."

Something registered in the back of Primer's eyes. He took in my statement and thought about it for a moment. "What are you talking about?" he asked.

I turned to Rusty and Dave who sat huddled in the car with me. "Can we talk inside?" I said more as a statement than a question. "What we have to share with you is too important to be passed on here."

"Like what?" Uncle Jude asked.

I sighed, adopting a tone like I was talking to a little child. "I told you, Jude, there are things about this Lost Chord that you don't know. Things that could save you life. And if you won't bring us inside to talk with you, I'm going to drive off and let you face the music yourself." I liked this last statement of mine. It was quite poetic. And it was a double entendre.

"All right." Jude said in exasperation. "Come inside.

All of you. And leave your keys in the car!" He began walking back up the front stairs to the entrance, motioning for us to follow him.

"What are you going to do?" Rusty said, before we got out of the car. "What are you going to tell him?"

"Trust me," I repeated. "I've gotten us this far haven't I?"

"Christopher," she said in a whispered breath, "You still don't have any idea what sort of man we're dealing with. He looks harmless, but I'm telling you he's a monster."

She had called me Christopher again. I wondered if I could get her to do that all the time. I liked it. But now was not the right setting to bring up that possibility. "Yeah, though I walk through the Valley of the Shadow of Death," I said, trying to lighten the mood.

"This is serious, Shade. I don't want to go in!" It was obvious that Rusty was terrified. And she was back to calling me Shade. What a dilemma. Dave was still sitting silently in the back seat.

"Come on kids, in unity there is strength," I smiled encouragingly. Uncle Jude was at the top of the stairs, signaling for us to come. I got out of the car, leaving my car keys in the ignition as requested, and began walking towards the stairs. I motioned for Rusty and Dave to join me. I saw them reluctantly get out of the car. First Rusty, then Dave. They followed me up the stairs into the entrance of the Ranch. I waited for them to catch up with me before I walked the eight steps up to the entrance door. Uncle Jude was already inside. The two guards were waiting at the bottom of the steps for us. Slowly, we began to walk up, with me in the lead by one step, and Rusty and Dave following. It felt like we were about to enter the jaws of some monstrous beast.

"Yeah, though I walk through the Valley of the Shadow of Death," I repeated.

"Stop it, Shade!" Rusty called from behind me. "This is no time for jokes."

She did not know how serious I was.

CHAPTER 10

Uncle Jude was waiting for us as we entered the front door of the ranch. The front door led into a large lobby with several wooden chairs and a sofa. We walked past that and followed Jude down a hallway. There were rooms upon rooms that we passed. Hallways that led to other hallways. I was immediately lost.

"Where are all the people?" I asked. Outside of the two guards, I hadn't seen a soul.

"They are in chapel," Uncle Jude curtly replied.

"Where's that?" I asked.

Uncle Jude pointed forward. "The chapel is a separate building."

"I didn't see any other buildings," I told him.

"It's behind the Ranch," he said. "That's where you should have parked, too. We like to keep the Ranch front clear."

"Why?" I asked.

"It looks nicer," he said.

"Oh," was my repartee. I'm quite witty when I want to be. Finally Uncle Jude stopped walking and entered a room. Rusty, Dave and I followed. So did the guards.

We were in the console room of a large recording studio. There was a couch and several padded black leather swivel chairs, as well as a couple of bar stools. Uncle Jude sat down on one of the chairs nearest the wall. I sat on another chair opposite him. Rusty and Dave sat together on the couch.

"Okay," Jude Primer said, "Talk".

I looked at the two burly bear-like guards who had been with us since we first arrived. "Are you sure you want Mutt and Jeff there to hear this?" I asked him.

"They are among my most trusted," Jude said. He pulled a cigarette from a pack that was lying on the console and then lit it. I was surprised. It didn't seem to go with the image of cult leader, but then again what did I know? I knew, however, that Uncle Jude was thinking, although I didn't know what he was thinking. I could almost smell the cogs burning as the wheels turned round in his head. Then he nodded to himself. "Okay," he called to the two guards, who despite the size of the console room, seemed to be having difficulty making themselves comfortable. They were standing around with their arms crossed. "Wait outside," he told them. They nodded together, almost in unity, and walked outside the console room.

Uncle Jude turned to me. "Okay," he said, blowing smoke in my face. "What is it that you've got to tell me about this Lost Chord?"

It was interesting. Since my third eye had been enhanced by my experience the day before, I truly believed my psychic ability had been accelerated. As we had been walking down the hallways of the Ranch, various images flashed in front of me. I saw all sorts of activities from people praying to people being tortured. I didn't know how much of it was my imagination, and how much of it I was receiving as a result of being in the vicinity of the Ranch.

Now, as I sat across from him, I saw different pictures in my mind. They were images of Uncle Jude in different guises: musician, lover, spiritual leader, sodomist, song writer, sadist, healer. These images spiraled across my consciousness. I didn't know if he was projecting them to me, or if I was just picking them up. I was sure they were real. They made me realize what a powerful and dangerous foe the man sitting opposite me was. I felt a shiver run from the base of my spine to the top of my head.

"The first thing I've got to tell you, Jude," I started to say very seriously, but paused. I was about to lay into him about stealing the Lost Chord, which he obviously had. Instead, something made me totally change my line of conversation. I skipped a beat then continued: "Is that this is a gorgeous studio." I pointed at the recording board. "What is this, a 32 track board?"

"48 tracks, actually," he said. His energy had suddenly shifted. "Fully automated and, of course, it's completely digital."

"Of course," I agreed. "This is incredible. This is one of the nicest studios I've seen. Particularly around these parts. We could be in L.A. right now, and I wouldn't know the difference."

"Thank you," he replied.

"And that's a remarkable effects mount," I said, pointing at a bank of echo, reverb and other studio processing equipment.

"Only the best," he said smiling. "Are you an engineer?"

"Nah," I said humbly. "Just a musician. Though I do

have a little 8 track at home. I play lead guitar with the Cosmic Blues Band. Dave here's our keyboard player. My name is Christopher Shade."

Jude tilted his head and then snapped his fingers as though remembering something. "Of course," he said excitedly, "I've seen you before. Down in Boulder. You're a good player, man. A very good player."

"Thank you," I said, even more humbly. My intuition had been right. Now, we were relating as musicians and not as cops and robbers. At least for the moment. It felt much better. "I've really enjoyed your music, too. Are you working on anything new?"

"You bet!" he said, perking up.

"Anything I can hear?" I asked.

"It's not finished quite yet," he said. Then he smiled and for a moment I saw the devil. "But when it is, believe me, you'll hear it."

Suddenly, I understood. And I was scared, really scared. I knew that with his talent and his connections, he could do it. He was going to somehow use part of the Lost Chord in his new music.

Just as quickly as we had begun the conversation about music, I stopped it. I did not know what was happening to me, nor how or why I was being directed in this manner. Nor did I know by whom. Suddenly, my cheeriness left me and I stared him straight in the eyes and said, "You can't do it, Jude."

"Do what?" he demanded. His eyes locked with mine and he knew that I knew. If I had had my psychic ability enhanced yesterday, his had probably been enhanced three decades ago. He was an extremely powerful man with a hypnotic voice, gesture and gaze. For a moment he began applying some form of psychic manipulation on me. I thought for a second that I was going to nod out because his energy was so strong. Then, I became aware of a pair of rainbow colored wings, and Uncle Jude's spell was broken.

"You know what I'm talking about," I said sternly. I looked back at Dave and Rusty, but they seemed somehow to be mesmerized. I didn't understand how, but not much was making sense at this point in time and space. I turned back to Jude. "You've got the Lost Chord. You stole it from her." I pointed at Rusty.

"I didn't steal anything!" Jude shouted angrily.

"Okay, then, Jay Lawson stole it from her and brought it to you," I replied forcefully. "And now you've got it. It strikes me that you are planning to use it for your next recording because you think that if this new record has the Lost Chord on it, it will be a big hit and you'll be famous and have money again." I shook my head in disgust. "Right?"

"I don't need any Lost Chord to make me rich and famous. I'm already rich and famous," he shouted.

"Yeah right," I said cynically. "When's the last time you made the Billboard Charts? 1975? '76? How many years ago, Jude?"

"I don't need to take this crap from you!" Jude screamed at me. "Some two bit guitar player telling Uncle Jude he's a has been?"

"I never said you were a has been," I answered. "I did think it, however!"

All the shouting had broken the hypnotic spell cast on Rusty and Dave. I heard her say, "You are a despicable human being, Jude Primer."

Uncle Jude turned from me. "Who the hell are you?" he asked.

"You raped her about ten years ago," I said calmly.

"I've never raped anyone!" Jude screamed. Saliva was dripping from his lip. It was not very attractive. It was, however, rather frightening.

"If you use the Lost Chord on your recording," I began, quickly trying to change the subject, "It could kill someone." I felt that the man was about to start pummeling us, me in particular, with his fists.

The words seemed to bring Uncle Jude back to some semblance of stability. "Doubtful," he said. "I've listened to it. It is certainly a monumental piece of sonic exploration, Miss," he said, suddenly honoring Rusty. "I've never experienced anything like it. At least anything that was electronically created. You've done you're homework well."

"Do you know what the Lost Chord is, Jude?" I asked in all seriousness.

"Of course," he replied. "It's like Jacob's Ladder, a stairway to heaven, using sound."

"Is that what happened to you?" I asked. "Did you go to heaven when you heard the sounds?"

"Naturally," Uncle Jude said matter of factly. "I've been there before. But I've never had the experience triggered so effectively by an artificial sound."

What did I have to lose? "Yeah," I began. "Well, I went there, too. Did you have any conversations with angels?"

He looked at me in puzzlement. "Angels?" he shook his head. "No, but I did see Christ, our Lord. He was beckoning for me to join him."

"And did you?" I asked.

"I couldn't!" he said, slamming his hand into the padded console.

"Why not?" I asked in a calming voice. Something was very wrong.

"Because I was in chains!" he screamed. Suddenly he began to cry. Very real tears poured down his face as he talked. "But the others, they said that this was as it should be, and that as soon as I made another hit record, our savior would see me again and forgive me for all my trespasses."

"What others?" I asked.

"Never mind," he said, as he began to wipe the tears from his face and regain his composure.

"No, it's important, Jude," I repeated. "What others?"

"The Dark Ones," Uncle Jude said. "The ones who are my friends. They tell me I am the new Messiah!" The words seemed to freeze the blood in my body.

"Oh Christ!" I heard Rusty mutter.

"I don't think so," I said. "The Dark Ones. Christ wasn't seeing him. Remember?"

"Shut up!" Jude shouted at me.

"Listen, Jude," I began. "I went to a place very similar to where you went." I doubted it was true. At least I hoped it wasn't. But at least it might make that connection again, as our brief musical truce had done.

"You did?" Jude said in awe.

"Yes," I continued. "I talked with an angel. The Angel of Sound, as a matter of fact. He told me that this Lost Chord was very dangerous, and that we had to be very careful about how it was used."

"Of course," Jude said. "I will be very careful."

"It's addictive," I said.

"I know that," Jude answered.

"It can knock people out of their bodies."

"Most definitely," he answered with a sardonic smile. "Don't you think I know that?"

"If someone were driving a car and heard the Lost Chord, just think what would happen."

"Don't worry," Jude said calmly. His personality changes were a little too abrupt for me. I was beginning to wonder if he was suffering from some sort of multiple personality disorder. "I wouldn't do that."

"Well, thank you!" I shouted. Maybe I had broken through.

"I don't want to kill people."

"Thank you!" I repeated.

"Give us back the Lost Chord!" I heard Rusty urge.

"No, I can't give it back. It must serve me," Jude said in that insanely calm voice. He was nodding to himself.

"How will it serve you?" Rusty asked. There was real panic in her voice.

"By allowing others to serve the new Messiah."

"I don't understand?" Rusty told him.

"I think I do," I said. I looked Jude directly in the eyes again, summoning as much of my will as possible, trying to get him to focus on me and not to drift into whatever la-la land he was now escaping to. "Jude!" I said, shaking him by the shoulders. "What are you going to do with the Lost Chord?"

Primer snapped back into his body. He was obviously used to drifting in and out of different dimensions rather quickly. I didn't know where he had been. I didn't care. What I wanted was an answer. He gave me one.

"True, I admit the Lost Chord is addictive," he began, picking up from a statement I had made to him minutes before this. The man was definitely not in balance. "In fact, I can hardly wait to get you worthless trash out of here so I can return to the bliss I was in before I was so rudely interrupted. But, it is not as dangerous as you think. I have already been experimenting with it. In fact, I am doing so at this moment in our chapel, with my fine students who are experiencing bursts of the Lost Chord—millisecond bursts."

"What?" Rusty, Dave and I screamed simultaneously.

"Yes," Jude answered. "I've had it piped into the chapel, underneath the music we normally use. It's coming in at sequences of half a second in length. Right now I have it programmed to repeat every fifteen seconds."

"And?" I asked nervously.

"Chapel normally lasts for an hour. It is a time of reflection and prayer. It starts at six o'clock in the morning, when my beloveds come to listen to my words, the words of their exalted master."

"Yeah," I said, waiting for the punch line.

"Look at you watch, my guitar playing friend."

"Shade," I said. "Christopher Shade."

"Look at your watch, Mr. Shade," Uncle Jude repeated. "What time is it?"

"Nearly eleven," I answered. Since there was a large wall clock in the studio, I thought that all these theatrics were ridiculous. Still, I waited for the punch line, which by now had been telegraphed, or telepathed, at least to me.

"They are still there," Primer said, laughing rather sardonically. "Even as we speak, they are still there. They can't leave. They are fully conscious, or at least as conscious as they ever have been, but they can't move. They don't know why they can't leave the chapel. Only I know. But they can't leave! They are stuck in time and space due to your most interesting Lost Chord. And I am their master. Soon my mastery will expand to envelope the world, for I am the new Messiah!"

"You're experimenting with it already?" I asked in disbelief.

"Of course," Uncle Jude replied. "The Lord helps those who help themselves."

"Where is Lawson?" Rusty asked.

"In the chapel, of course," Uncle Jude sardonically replied. "Would you like to see him?"

CHAPTER 11

The chapel was a geodesic dome directly behind the Ranch. It was approximately 100 feet in diameter. There was a covered stairwell, with glass on the sides and ceiling, attaching the chapel to the Ranch, although it was obviously a separate unit.

Uncle Jude was leading the party, followed by me, Rusty, Dave and the two guards. No one said anything as we walked from the studio, which was apparently on the left wing of the Ranch to the geodesic dome. Rusty, Dave and I did exchange some rather incredulous looks with each other as we walked.

I guess they were depending upon me to continue as front man for the group. "Trust me!" I had mouthed to Rusty at one point during the walk. I wanted to see where Jude was going. I wanted to see the chapel. I wanted to see his followers and to see Jay Lawson. Then, suddenly, about ten feet before we had reached the chapel, warning bells began to go off in my head.

"No!" I shouted, and stopped moving. Rusty and Dave looked at each other, puzzled by my outburst. They continued walking. "Don't go in!" I shouted.

"What's the matter?" Uncle Jude asked. "You wanted to come here." He stood at the door, which was opened. He beckoned Rusty and Dave inside. They looked at him. Then at me.

I had been having a confusing time, to say the least, with my enhanced psychic powers. I had been getting warnings ever since Jude suggested that we go to the chapel. But the warnings screamed at me with intense clarity right before we were to enter the chapel. I guess I had been ignoring these feelings of dread when they had begun in the studio. It was only when I heard a voice say, "Don't go in there! He will make you his slaves as well!" that I really understood.

I don't know who the voice was or where it was coming from inside my head. But it was as loud as any real voice I'd ever heard. It was just a little bit too late. By the time I tried to warn Dave and Rusty, they were already in the field of the frequencies. As they stood at the open door to the chapel, the Lost Chord had them.

Dave and Rusty had turned their back to me and were walking, zombie like, into the chapel. I was still 10 feet away. The sonics of the Lost Chord were not affecting me. I was about to run in the opposite direction when the two guards grabbed me, one on each side.

"Let me go you bums!" I yelled at them. It was obvious that they didn't hear me. Ear plugs! Uncle Jude had this all planned. They continued walking toward the chapel with me between them. Then, the two of them pushed me in and slammed the door behind me.

There were over thirty people in the chapel, a mixture of men and women. They were dressed in the casual style of Colorado, with lots of denims and plaids. And typical of the Boulder area, there was also a lot of purple and turquoise. Most of the people were sitting cross legged in states of deep meditation. None of them were moving very much. Occasionally, a man or a woman would scratch themselves or stretch a bit. I don't think they had noticed Rusty, Dave or me enter the room.

There was a thick smell of incense in the room. There were hardwood floors and lots of picture windows with a view of the Indian Peaks mountain range. Photos and paintings of Uncle Jude were everywhere. He was dressed mostly in a white suit in those images. Sometimes, he appeared wearing what looked like purple sweats. There were even a few shots of him in dark robes. He looked good: all loving and gentle. It was nice and warm in the chapel. Very pretty music was coming from a high quality speaker system. It sounded like Uncle Jude. I had never realized he was that talented.

It felt so good in the chapel, very comfortable and relaxing. I decided to join Dave and Rusty, who were already sitting cross legged on some pillows on the floor. I was feeling very good. That's the only way I can describe it. I was slightly sleepy and feeling just a little bit stoned. But I was fully conscious and experiencing a delightful sensation of being at peace with the world and myself. I looked around the chapel. Most of the people had their eyes closed. But one, a woman with dark hair, had her eyes open. We looked at each other and smiled. A feeling of love was exchanged between us—it was wonderful. And then, a wave of love for Uncle Jude passed between us. It was also wonderful.

Time was without meaning for me. How long I sat cross legged on the floor was impossible to tell. It could have been seconds. It might have been hours. It didn't matter. Nothing mattered. I just felt so good.

Then, Shamael came to me.

"Stop it!" I heard his deep voice say, and I knew who it was.

"What do you want?" I thought. "Leave me alone. I'm happy."

"You are intoxicated by the frequencies that you sought to reclaim!" the voice answered. In my mind's eye, I saw the gigantic Angel of Sound once more. We were together in the same temple where I had first met him. Yet, at the same time, I could feel myself being in Uncle Jude's chapel. I was in two places at one time. How interesting.

"Leave me alone," I said to the angel.

"We can not directly interfere," Shamael said. "We can only guide. As your guide, we suggest you end this condition and remove yourself from this place. Otherwise, you will be enslaved for the rest of your life."

"Enslaved?" I asked. "What do you mean?"

"Do you wish to be like this for the rest of your life?" he asked.

"Like what?" I asked. As I did, I saw myself looking at myself sitting in the chapel. I was still sitting in the chapel and still talking to Shamael. I was in three places at one time. Even more interesting.

"Oh God!" I said in all three of my bodies, as I realized where I was, and why I was and what was happening. From one of those dimensions, I looked at Shamael and said, "Please help me!"

Shamael touched me gently on the third eye. Suddenly, I was back in my body, sitting cross-legged on the floor of the chapel. I felt stiff and hungry and I realized that I had to go to the bathroom.

"Whew!" I said. The music was still on, but now it was only old Uncle Jude singing in that nasty twang of his, and he still seemed second rate to me. I could not believe that I had been so powerfully affected and controlled by this rather terrible music. It was obvious that somehow the Lost Chord frequencies—at least the sporadic Lost Chord frequencies which Jude Primer was experimenting with in the chapel, were no longer affecting me as they had.

"Come on!" I said to Rusty and Dave who were in front of me.

Neither one of them responded.

"Come on!" I repeated, this time tapping lightly on Dave's shoulder.

Dave turned around and looked at me with soporific eyes. "Please stop doing that," he said in a gentle but firm voice. Then he turned away from me.

"Dave, come on!" I said. I tapped him again. He didn't respond.

"Rusty," I hissed. "Come out of it!" I tapped her shoulder, rather roughly I admit.

"Leave me alone," she said in that same gentle, but firm voice. "Or I will have to have one of the guards remove you."

"Rusty," I said, still trying to keep my voice down, but definitely verging on the edge of panic with my tone. "It's the Lost Chord. It's got you. You have to fight it. You can't give in!"

But I realized that she could give in, as I had given in. There wasn't a thing I could do about it. Or was there?

I stood up and quietly walked around to face Rusty. She is a very pretty lady with natural red hair and a pale, clear complexion. At that moment, her eyes were closed and she looked positively beatific. Then, I gently touched her on her forehead as the angel had done to me.

Rusty opened her eyes and looked at me. "Stop that will you! I'm very happy here, Shade. Now why don't you just go away before I call one of those guards."

"Rusty!" I said. "Please, Rusty!" She had closed her eyes again. I was about to try another third eye tap when I heard another voice.

"Leave quickly!" it said. That deep internal voice. Was it Shamael? Was it an aspect of Christopher? Whoever it was, I took the hint. My bones creaked as I stood up and made my way through one of the side doors of the chapel. This one led directly outside, and not back to the Ranch.

I walked through the outside door of the chapel and was immediately hit by a blast of cold Colorado mountain air. It felt good. It was also dark outside, which gave me an indication that I had been in the chapel for at least seven hours. Whew! I was in back of the Ranch now. There had been a lot more activity normally carried on here than I would have suspected. There was a huge dumpster and loading ramps into what probably was a kitchen. There were a number of automobiles, including my own. How convenient for me. They must have moved the Bronco in order to get it out of the way of the front.

No one else was around. Nevertheless, I was very stealthful in my maneuvering to my Bronco. I didn't want anyone to see me. I didn't want to have a tussle with a 300 pound bear posing as a human. I wanted to go home and go to bed, and try to think this thing through. I felt scared and lost and I wished that Dave and Rusty were here with me. My bladder was really full. I relieved myself and then thought for a moment. What could I do?

Here was a madman who had a new toy and knew

how to use it. My God, did he know how to use it! I was alone without the two people who could have probably helped me figure out what to do. I felt desperate and totally deserted.

The doors to the Bronco were open and the keys were in the ignition. I started the vehicle and drove around the back entrance of the complex to the circular driveway where I had previously parked. Then, I drove down the driveway towards the road. Escape seemed easy enough. Of course, the electrified fence could have been a deterrent, had I been thinking that clearly. But, I was not. I just wanted to go home.

When I saw that eight foot fence with the gate closed and found myself approaching it in my trusty Bronco, the only thing I could think to do was to speed up. The Bronco hit that fence going 55 miles per hour and, outside of a slight impact and a little crackle, I hardly felt a thing. I guess the fence was designed to keep people on the outside from coming in, not stop people on the inside from going out—especially if they were driving cars. Maybe too many people were intimidated by electrified fences. I don't know, but it wasn't bad, believe me.

Then, I was on the dirt road leading back to 72 without a plan or a prayer. I didn't know what to do. I didn't know where to go. I was scared and I was stunned. I just wanted a hot bath and my bed, and maybe a beer. No! I wanted to play my guitar. I wanted to be back at the club, gigging at the Dugout. Gigging! I looked at the clock in my vehicle. It read 7:45. We had a gig tonight!

Then I did one of the more illogical things in my life. I say illogical, because depending on all the various experiences and situations that were occurring in my life, you would have thought that missing a gig at the Dugout would have been no big thing. But, for some reason it was a big thing; it was a very big thing. I should have gone to bed, or to the police, or done something more in alignment with my day's experiences. Instead, as I headed down the Canyon toward Boulder, I knew I had to make the gig at the club. With or without Dave, with or without Rusty, I had to make the gig at the Dugout.

Suddenly, I knew I was safe.

CHAPTER 12

Sometimes playing music can bring you back home, more so than crawling into bed or taking a hot bath. The last couple of days had brought me face to face with the real and rather amazing power of sound and its ability to change consciousness. I'd been pulled out of my body and had a one on one with an angelic being. I'd faced a mad-man guru who had thus far successfully enslaved two dear friends of mine. I'd had my body and my psyche pushed beyond their normal limits. Yet, that night at the Dugout, I felt fine.

Talk about the healing power of music! Maybe that was why my inner guidance had directed me towards the gig and not towards home and bed. My real home was with music, and in particular, playing music. Always has been, always will be. If you put a guitar in my hand (preferably electric) and we play the right tune, I can be suffering and forget about the pain. I can just have had my heart ripped out from inside of me and feel nothing but the music. I can just have encountered an angel and a madman and feel just fine.

I did that night! We performed as a threesome. It had been quite sometime since that had happened. I think the last time was when Bill, our bass player, was ill, and Dave had to cover for him on keyboards and play his parts. It wasn't magic then. It was now. We were a little lightweight in the rhythm section when it was my turn to solo, but outside of that, the sound wasn't that different—except for my playing. From a very detached and objective viewpoint, I can honestly report that it was sensational. Perhaps it was because my soul was screaming with pain—I don't really know, but my playing was exceptional. The pain I experienced within me was reflected and even amplified in the cry of my guitar. And that night, while I performed, I was able to release all the sadness and the sorrow and the exhaustion and the confusion. My notes dripped with an anguish beyond words, revealed in the very sounds my fingers brought forth from the Stratocaster.

I remember a number of times catching Tony and Bill exchanging glances of disbelief during my solos. It was as though the spirit of Jimi Hendrix was coming through me. And you know— maybe that was so. I don't know. I was playing things I'd only dreamed of before, bending notes and shaking my vibrato with an energy I didn't know I had in me.

I was pulling songs from my past that I hadn't played in many years, and playing them perfectly. I remembered the words and everything. It was as though I was finding myself and affirming myself and my life through the music I had known. "Voodoo Chile", the extended version from *Electric Ladyland*, wailed through the club for nearly a half hour. My fingers were on fire. It wasn't the blues. But then, it wasn't exactly not the blues, and the audience loved it. My playing was hot. My singing was hot. People were going crazy.

I didn't say anything to Bill and Tony about what had happened. At least not yet. I didn't know what I was going to say. The whole experience was so complicated that I just wanted to escape. I told them that Dave was sick and that we could make it as a threesome that night. As soon as we started playing, they didn't ask me anything more. I really like Bill and Tony. They are excellent human beings. And I had no hesitation about turning to them for help. It was just that for a short time at least, I needed to get away from everything that had happened. The only way that I knew how to do that was through my music.

Sometime during the second set, the American Indian came in. I was in the middle of a fiery solo and still somehow he caught my eye as he walked in the door. We locked eyes for a moment, and then I was back in the sweet ecstasy of my playing. It had been spooky. He looked at me as our eyes met. Then, he just nodded, as though he knew me and was just dropping by to pay his respects. I'd never seen him before in my life; yet from that first moment, I knew our paths were to be inexorably crossed.

He was big, probably six two or six three. Clean shaven (how many Indians have beards) with long black hair braided into a ponytail. He must have weighed two hundred and fifty pounds easily. He was very stocky, but not fat. He was dressed in jeans and a denim coat, which did not supply much warmth considering the temperature outside. But he didn't seem to be bothered.

He sat at the bar after he came in. From time to time I'd notice him, feeling a pull towards him that I couldn't understand. He seemed to be about my age, but I couldn't tell since he was pretty far away and the club was not well lit. During the break, I passed by him on the way to the bathroom. Again, he nodded at me in recognition. I nodded back at him. On the way back from the bathroom he motioned me over.

Up close, I could see that he was older than me, with deep furrows in his brow and a long, hooked nose. He had piercing brown eyes that seemed to penetrate down to my inner being. It was scary. I couldn't wait to get back on stage and start playing again.

"How you doing, man?" I said as casually and as coolly as I could. After all, I was the star at the Dugout that night. I had to be cool, at least for a while.

"I dreamed you," is all he said.

"Dreaming's a groove," I said back to him in my rock n' roll guise.

"I dreamed you," he said again.

"What?" I said, putting a hand to my ear. The jukebox was loud and I was pretending that I hadn't heard him properly. But I had. Believe me, I had. I just didn't want to be in that space then.

"We will talk later," he answered, motioning back to the stage. I got an orange juice from the bartender, still exchanging stares with the Indian. I wasn't drinking alcohol that night, so juice seemed the best. Then, I went back to the small stage riser area where we were performing for one last set.

I really wished someone had taped that night. Once in a while, someone (usually a member of the band, but sometimes a member of the audience) will record us. And usually, it's pretty good. The recording, I mean, not necessarily the playing. I have this belief that the better the playing, the worse the recording's going to be, and vice versa. If it's a normal night with ordinary playing, you'll get a pretty good sounding recording. If it's a terrible night and our playing really stinks, you'll get a fabulous recording. And, if it's a magical night, as it was that night, either the recording equipment will go up in smoke, or no one will record. This has been my experience for the last 15 years, and I believe it is true.

I remember reading once about some musicologists who went to record some aboriginal people performing a sacred ceremony. They had all the latest high tech equipment, but they did not have the permission of the people they were recording. After the ceremony was over, they played back the recording. It was blank. I think I remember reading, or hearing about the same thing with Tibetan monks who were being recorded. The point is that sound, as I was beginning to understand, could be magical. And, I guess when you're dealing with magic, you want the blessings of the spirits.

Anyway, the rest of the night continued to be magic, so of course nobody recorded it. It's just as well. I have these incredible memories of some of the songs just soaring out of me, although I admit that much of our set list is actually lost somewhere in my consciousness. I know we did a couple of old Cream songs, and even a Stones song or two, along with the usual numbers like "Hootchie Kootchie Man", "The Thrill Is Gone" and "I Just Want to Make Love to You". I think maybe we even did a version of "Dear Mr. Fantasy", although I'm not sure. Reality was getting to be very fluid. By the end of the set, I was ready to talk with the Indian.

Incidentally, please don't think I'm prejudiced if I sometimes call this guy an Indian. I'm simply ignorant about the right terminology. I just don't know what the politically correct term is these days. It used to be American Indian. Then it became Native American, but I'm not really sure now. Since I didn't know his tribe, I couldn't call him a Hopi or a Lakota. As a matter of fact, I recall that I was once involved in a conversation with a couple of Lakotas talking at a bar, and they referred to each other as "Indians". I guess it depends on who's doing the talking and who's doing the listening. But forgive me if my lack of a politically correct language bothers anyone. It is not my intention to do so. Really.

By the end of our third and last set, I was totally flying. I knew I was exhausted, but at the same time I was on an adrenaline, or maybe an endorphin high that truly had me out there. I packed up my guitar while a few of the audience members came over to compliment me on my playing. I glanced up and saw that the Indian was still waiting for me. He was nursing a Coke, probably the same one he had had earlier that night. He was now stripped down to a black tee-shirt, his denim jacket on the seat next to him.

I walked over to him with my guitar case in my hand. I knew we needed to talk, but the Dugout had already done last call, and I figured we would probably have to go somewhere else.

Again, we nodded at each other. "Christopher Shade," I said, holding out my right hand.

"Charlie Singing Eagle," he said, taking my hand in his and shaking it. "Very nice playing".

"Thank you very much," I said humbly. I was good at being humble about compliments. I didn't receive them very well, but I liked to hear them, nevertheless. It was an interesting paradox.

"I dreamed you," he said for the third time that evening.

"I know," I said. "I heard you before."

"Why did you act like you didn't?" he asked.

"Because I didn't want to get into it then. I do now."

"Do you know what I'm talking about?" he asked.

"No," I said with a smile. "But, I'm interested in hearing about it."

"Good," he replied.

"Should we go over to Penny Lane and have a coffee?" I asked.

"Good," he said again. I was afraid this guy Charlie was going to be a little limited in the conversation department.

"Come on," I told him. He followed me out the door of the Dugout and then to my car, where I stowed my guitar in the back.

Penny Lane was about seven blocks down Pearl Street. We could have driven, but I thought the walk would do me some good. It was open late at night and you could get a really fine cup of coffee. It was also very big on ambience.

"Let's go," I said.

"Do you believe in spirits?" he asked as we walked down Pearl Street.

"Why?" I asked.

"Because there's a big old medicine man standing right next to you. It might be Black Elk. I don't know yet. He hasn't spoken. He's been with you all night," Charlie said, as we walked down the street.

"Anyone else there?" I asked rather humorously.

"Oh yes!" Charlie replied with certainty. "Jimi Hendrix was around you, too, while you were playing. Now he's gone. I guess he moved on."

"Guess so," I said scratching my head. Jimi Hendrix standing around me while I was playing? I think if I hadn't been so tired I would have found the conversation comical, or just totally absurd. I wasn't sure which.

"And who is that big archangel standing behind you?" Charlie asked in amazement.

"What!" I exclaimed. "You can see him?" I asked back, equally in amazement.

"Can't miss him," Charlie replied. "He's huge."

I breathed out a heavy sigh. It was getting to be one in the morning. I had been up since eight. I'd faced a madman, lost my friends, played maybe the best set of my life, and now I was going to have coffee with a clairvoyant Indian. I knew it was going to be a long night.

CHAPTER 13

Penny Lane is an interesting place. No matter what time you go in, whether it's at three in the afternoon, eight at night, or as it was, one in the morning, there are always people in there. People, at best, is a euphemism. One friend of mine described Penny Lane as like being in the cantina scene in *Star Wars* where all the extra-terrestrials hang out. This is the second reference I've made to that movie, and you'd think it was one of my favorites. It is, but that's besides the point. I guess George Lucas must have really tapped into some archetypes. I mean, I haven't mentioned *King Kong* once yet, and that's also one of my favorite films, full of archetypes as well. Somehow, Skull Island didn't seem to be quite as appropriate a reference to Penny Lane—at least I hadn't noticed any 50 foot gorillas yet. But, the night was still young and considering how things were going, I couldn't be sure of anything.

The people who frequent Penny Lane are either students, artists, or beings from other dimensions who need a place to go where they won't stick out. It's not ordinarily frequented by men in three piece business suits, but to tell you the truth, there aren't too many of them in Boulder, anyway.

So, the image of a long haired rock n' roller with a head band wearing sunglasses talking with an enormous Indian in the middle of the night was not too strange for Penny Lane. In fact, it was rather ordinary.

Charlie Singing Eagle and I both picked up house coffees from the counter. I paid. Despite the hour, the place was filled with people, but there were still a few empty tables. Charlie pointed to a table in the back near the restrooms. I nodded. We walked to the table and then sat down opposite each other.

Charlie looked around. "Crowded," he remarked.

"You're not from around here are you?" I asked.

"Nope," he said. "Just visiting. I live in Arizona."

"Nice there," I said. I was not much for casual conversation. I could tell Charlie wasn't either.

"It's okay," he said.

"What tribe are you from?" I asked.

"I was born Lakota up in Pineridge, South Dakota, but I left the rez early."

"Are you a medicine man?" I inquired.

"Not officially," Charlie answered. "I know some medicine though."

I bet you do, I thought.

"What're you doing around these parts?" I continued questioning.

"Visiting," he answered.

"Oh," I said. I had more or less run out of questions, except for one. "When did you dream me?"

"Last night," he said.

"Convenient," I remarked. "Tell me about it."

Charlie nodded. "I was with Grandma Gladys. We were meditating together. We saw you. We could tell that you needed my help."

"Grandma Gladys?" I asked.

"My teacher," he replied. "She lives up in the mountains."

As he spoke of Grandma Gladys, I closed my eyes for a moment and saw a vision of an ancient woman, of Native American origin. She was old and gnarled with long white hair and she radiated incredible light. Then, I was back at Penny Lane.

"I see," I responded. Then after pausing for a few seconds, I asked, "Why did I need your help?"

"I don't know," Charlie answered. "It's got something to do with sound. I work with sound."

"Oh you do?" I said, not at all surprised.

Charlie nodded his head. "I've studied with the Lakotas, the Hopi, the Sufis, the Tibetans—all different traditions. Even some Kabbalistic Rabbis!" he said with a wink.

"Interesting combination," I remarked.

"Yes," he acknowledged. "But at the same time, all the same, for sound comes from one source—the Creator. All the various traditions are different wave forms, or aspects of the Creator. But they are one."

I nodded my head. "Yes, that's right, and very succinctly put, too."

"Thank you," he said. "Words are important. Sounds are even more important."

"So, what was I doing in the dream?" I asked.

"It wasn't really a dream," Charlie said. "That's what I call it. Like I said, I was meditating."

"I get that," I replied.

"Anyway," Charlie continued. "When I saw you, you were playing in that club, the Dugout. That's how I knew to come there."

"Interesting," I said. "But what gave you the impression I was in trouble. My playing was pretty good tonight," I continued, a smile on my face.

"It wasn't you that told me," Charlie said. "It was that big angel. Who is that guy anyway? I've never seen him before. Neither had Grandma Gladys. She was pretty impressed with him though. Pretty impressed with you, too, for having him around. That's why I'm here. She sent me. Otherwise I'd still be in the mountains with her."

"But you had this vision," I interjected, "This meditation or dream."

"I have plenty of dreams," he responded. "I don't always act on them. I usually don't, as a matter of fact. Grandma Gladys was pretty insistent that I come to you. That's why I'm here."

"Thanks," I replied.

"No problem," he answered. Then we were silent for a few minutes as I tried to sort out what was happening. I didn't know who to trust. I was feeling pretty paranoid lately. Still, there was something about this Indian, Charlie Singing Eagle, and about his teacher, Grandma Gladys, that made me feel better.

"What can I do to help?" Charlie asked.

My logical mind told me to keep my mouth shut, but my intuitive mind told me differently.

"Okay," I began. "Here's what's happened."

CHAPTER 14

I had never expected to hear an Indian say, "Sounds like bad medicine", but those are the words that Charlie Singing Eagle said once I finished telling him the story. He was not one to mince words, and what he said was accurate. I did, however, momentarily feel like I was in a grade C Western.

"Actually, it's bad sound medicine," I countered.

Charlie looked at me and shook his head. "You have some sense of humor, Christopher."

"Some folks think I'm kind of funny."

Charlie didn't say anything, probably out of politeness. We had been sitting for over an hour while I told my story, and we'd each gone through 3 cups of coffee. It was after two in the morning and I had a strange caffeine buzz.

"But you're right," Charlie said. "It is bad sound medicine. I occasionally travel to places similar to where you met that angel."

"I bet you do."

"Yes, but I do it through chanting and meditation, not through listening to a computerized recording like this Lost Chord. My traveling is the result of years of discipline. I'm not even sure that most people should have access to the realms you're talking about."

"Maybe not," I agreed. "But the Lost Chord is here, now. For some reason, it's manifested on the earth plane through the work of my friend, Rusty."

"Who now may be a zombie in the hands of a cult fascist!" Charlie added. "A lot of good it's done her."

"Things got out of control," I replied.

"Quickly, too," Charlie countered. "I have nothing against science. I'm a big fan of understanding the truth, but I think we've reached a time when we can scientifically create more than we know how to handle."

"Amen," I said.

"Mitaquiasi," Charlie said.

"What's that mean?" I asked.

"The same thing," he said. "Loosely translated it means 'all my relations', but we use it for the same effect."

"Gotcha." Then, there was a long period of silence. I had run out of things to say and so had Charlie. We were both deeply immersed in thought. I was thinking about Rusty and Dave and wondering what we could possibly do.

"So, what are we going to do?" I finally asked, still trying to figure out something and not succeeding very well.

"Rescue your friends, get the Lost Chord back, and pray that we don't get killed," Charlie said matter of factly.

"Are you the cavalry?" I asked.

"Do I look like the cavalry, white man?" Charlie snorted with a wide grin.

"What's the plan?"

"I've got some ideas," he said, nodding his head. "The spirits have already been giving me suggestions. I do know that from what you've told me, the sooner we get up to the Ranch and take care of business the better it will be. This Uncle Jude seems like he's already taking his own course of action and not waiting around."

"That's the truth!" I chimed in.

"So, we've got to get up there now and attempt to take control before things really get out of hand."

"It's the middle of the night," I said.

"We have work to do," he replied.

"Like what?"

"Did your friend Rusty make copies of the Lost Chord?" Charlie asked.

"I think so," I answered.

"Where are they?"

"At her condo, I guess."

"We have to go there," Charlie said.

"Why?" I asked.

"Maybe we can fight fire with fire," he replied.

"What do you mean?" I asked.

"You got any sort of portable sound playback system?" Charlie asked.

"Sure. I've got a ghetto blaster at home. Maybe Rusty's got one as well. Matter of fact, I think Dave once borrowed one of hers for a gig."

"Good," Charlie said. "If your friend Rusty has copies of this Lost Chord at her place, maybe we can make a cassette copy and use it as our ally at Uncle Jude's Ranch."

I was beginning to get the picture. "Brilliant!" I said. "We could pick up some ear plugs at an all night drug store and then use the Lost Chord against Uncle Jude."

"Something like that," Charlie said.

"Only one problem," I sighed.

"What's that?"

"The Lost Chord is on a computer. I'm really cyber challenged. I don't know anything about computers."

Charlie laughed. "Leave that to me."

With that, we departed Penny Lane, walking silently back to where I'd left my vehicle. Then, we were off in my Bronco towards Rusty's. Charlie proved to be an ingenious man. He opened Rusty's front door with a credit card, letting us into her place in the middle of the night. Then, he turned on her computer and in a matter of minutes, he had found the Lost Chord program. I knew enough about electronics to be able to hook up a cassette recorder to Rusty's computer system. I found a blank chrome tape and in a short time we were recording forty five minutes of the Chord onto a cassette

"That much time really isn't necessary," I pointed out to Charlie. "Five minutes will do."

"I'm not taking any chances," Charlie answered. "And someday, you know, I would like to try the Lost Chord myself," he said, pointing to the cassette recorder as we watched the VU meters. "I'm not against science, and this seems fascinating."

"Yeah," I said, answering both statements at the same time. It was obvious that with his computer skills Charlie knew a thing or two, and the Lost Chord was no doubt fascinating, to say the least.

Then, I found a reasonably good portable cassette player amidst all of Rusty's equipment. It was the one Dave had borrowed for a gig onetime and I knew it worked okay. There were no batteries, but we'd stop and get those at the same place where we'd find ear plugs.

I went back to watching the cassette recorder as it received the sounds of the Lost Chord. Charlie and I waited in silence until the machine was finished recording. Then, it was necessary to find out if the information had been picked up on the tape. There was only one way to do it. I rewound the tape to the beginning.

"Turn it off after ten seconds," I said, placing the headphones on my head. Then, I hit the start button of the cassette deck. The next thing I knew Charlie was shaking me.

"Where'd you go?" he asked, taking the headphones off me.

"I don't remember," I said. "I think I feel asleep. How long was I out for?"

"That thing is very powerful!" Charlie exclaimed. "You had barely put those headphones on when suddenly you zonked out in that chair."

"Want to try it?" I asked.

"Not this time," he answered. "You okay to drive?"

I nodded my head. "Yeah, sure, but I have to admit I'm a little tired. Can you drive a standard?" I asked, pulling out my Bronco keys.

Charlie laughed. He took the keys from my hand and put them in his pocket. "Anything else?" he asked.

"Not that I can think of."

"Let's go," Charlie said, picking up the portable stereo and slipping the cassette with the Lost Chord into his pocket.

As I had hoped, the all night pharmacy had both ear plugs and batteries. We got the best ear plugs and batteries that we could find. In the parking lot of the pharmacy, we put the batteries in the stereo and we put on the Lost Chord. I was hit by a slight feeling of euphoria, but it was nothing like the full effect of the sound.

I turned the stereo off. "Looks like it works," I said.

Charlie was shaking his head. "Pretty powerful, even with the ear plugs."

"Yes," I said, "but you should try the real thing."

"Someday," he said.

We were off again, this time up the mountain. Charlie drove. I tried to catch a quick nap in the back seat. I was exhausted and wanted more than anything to be home in bed. Yet, I knew he was right— the more time Uncle Jude had to work with the Lost Chord, the more dangerous the situation would be.

I thought about Rusty and Dave and the Chord, and Uncle Jude, and Charlie, and Shamael, and even Grandma Gladys whom I had not met. Then I feel asleep.

CHAPTER 15

"The world was created through sound!" Shamael said.

I nodded my head and watched as he waved his hand. I saw the creation of the earth and the planets, of suns and galaxies, and universes.

"It is not sound as you would think of in human terms. You think of sound as that which you perceive through your sense of hearing. Everything in the universe is in a state of vibration and has its own natural frequency. Everything in the universe was created from these frequencies, which are unique and natural to themselves," the angel continued.

"From the spinning of your electrons as they revolve around the nucleus of your atom, to the rotation of the planets around your sun, all these create vibrations which may be understood as being sound. They produce the sound, and they are the result of the sound. This is important. Do you understand?"

"I do, Shamael," I said. "Everything is in a state of vibration."

"That is so," the angel acknowledged. "You are nothing more or less than vibration. Your physical body, etheric bodies and other bodies are merely vibrating at different speeds, or different rates of being. It is important to learn to be able to consciously change the vibrations of these different bodies in order to be able to acclimate to the different frequency shifts that are occurring on your planet now. Do you understand?"

"I think so," I answered.

The angel waved his hand again and suddenly I was looking at myself, or rather looking at my selves, myriad versions of me all vibrating at various speeds. It was fairly awe-inspiring and rather complicated to understand.

"This is what your Lost Chord does. This is how it creates a gateway that allows dimensional access." Shamael touched my forehead and I was back as one being talking to the angel in that domed temple, standing next to a marble pillar and a fountain with luminescent liquid flowing from it. "These gateways have been accessed before by humans, particularly those who have devoted their lives to the sacred. They have worked with both the frequency of an object and its intention."

"Its intention?" I asked.

"When the Creator first spoke that word which brought illumination to the Universe, the Creator did not merely say 'Light', or the Divine equivalent of this."

"No?" I said, still trying to follow.

"No," Shamael repeated. "The Creator thought of the energy and of the intention of light, and then encoded this energy and intention upon the sound."

"Oh," I said, still not comprehending.

"A sound may be encoded with an intention, an energy or a thought form. It also may simply be a sound. When it becomes encoded with an intention, it becomes more powerful. When the Tibetan Monks on your planet chant one of their sacred mantras, they are not merely chanting words which create a frequency. They are also encoding the words with intentions. They do this through precise visualizations. This allows them to gain interdimensional access to various places. This creates the gateways."

"I understand this," I said.

"Through repeating these mantras, which by their very nature are sacred, and then adding visualizations to them, the Tibetans are able to make their mantras more powerful. The mantras become encoded with specific energy. By chanting previously encoded words such as these mantras, an uninitiated person may experience some of this gateway effect and perhaps travel to other realms of consciousness. The very act of repeating a mantra creates an intentionality. Nevertheless, discipline is required for continued clarification of the process. There is a built in protection in self-created sounds which does not allow those working with it to go beyond their own abilities."

All of a sudden, I began to understand what the angel was talking about. I nodded my head. "The Lost Chord does not require any intention or any discipline in order to work."

"Exactly," Shamael affirmed. "Through the transformation of the mantric formulae into sonic formulae, your friend has created an acceleration in the machinations of the universe. As has been said, this has happened before. It will happen again. But the Lost Chord is able to create the gateways without the conscious intention of the individual using it. Because of this, it can be manipulated by any who have knowledge of this process."

Uncle Jude, I thought.

"Exactly," said Shamael.

"But how can I stop him?" I asked aloud.

"You do not need to stop him. He will stop himself, but you must be part of that process."

"I don't understand?" I exclaimed.

"Only experience will reveal this truth," Shamael said. Suddenly, I woke up.

I had been asleep in the rear seat of my Bronco. I was covered by the blanket which I kept in the back to put over my guitar. I rubbed my eyes and looked up. It was getting light. I looked at my watch and saw it was after 6:00 am. Charlie Singing Eagle was not in the car, and I didn't have a clue as to where we were.

I sat up and stretched. We were somewhere out in the woods, that much was clear. There was a little cabin about 50 feet from where the car was parked. I got out and began walking towards it. A light was burning inside and I could hear voices.

"Here he comes now," I heard Charlie say as I walked up four steps to the cabin.

I entered the wooden cabin. It was a tiny A-frame made mostly of logs. There was a fire burning in the fireplace which cast long shadows over the two figures sitting in front of it. One of the figures was Charlie who was sitting on an old lounge chair. The other figure sitting in a wooden rocker I knew instantly.

"Christopher," Charlie said, "This is Grandma Gladys Goodnight."

I walked over to the tiny woman sitting with a blanket wrapped around her. "How do you do, ma'am?" I asked. She was the oldest looking woman I think I'd ever seen. Her entire face was one huge set of wrinkles. She had the clearest eyes I've ever seen and light seemed to radiate around her.

"Just fine, Christopher," she laughed, her eyes twinkling. "Did you have a good sleep."

"Excellent," I responded.

"Well, I believe you needed it after what you've been through," she said.

"I guess so." I answered.

"Pull up a chair and sit down with us," she stated.

"I'd love to ma'am," I said, as humbly as I could. "But I don't think we've got time." I looked at Charlie. "I thought you said it was urgent we get to the Ranch."

"It is, Christopher," Charlie said. "But it's even more urgent that we get some advice from Gladys."

I shook my head and yawned.

"Get the boy some coffee, Charlie!" Grandma Gladys said. "Sit down, boy!" She motioned to a stool that was next to her.

"Coffee?" Charlie asked me.

I shrugged my shoulders. "Sure. Why not?"

Charlie walked over to a pot of coffee that was sitting next to the fire. He poured me a cup and handed it to me. I thanked him and sat on the stool. Then I turned to the old woman, "Any advice you can spare?" I asked. "Anything that could help me out of this situation? I don't know how much Charlie has told you but....".

Grandma Gladys held up her hand and looked directly into my eyes. Her own eyes seemed to penetrate my being, down to the essence of my soul. "I know enough to tell you that there are some very powerful spirits involved in this situation of yours," she said firmly. "Not all of them are very good either. You can use every bit of help you can get."

"That's for sure," I confirmed.

Gladys looked at me and shook her head. "You've sure been through a lot of changes in the last few days."

"That's for sure," I said, again. I was beginning to sound like a broken record.

"A quick initiation in the spirit world," she offered.

"I guess you could say that," I affirmed.

"It is a good and powerful experience you have had."

I nodded my head. "That doesn't make it any easier."

"Easy is not the answer," she said. "Truth is."

I liked this old lady. There was something very comforting about the words she spoke and her wisdom. Still, I was scared.

"I'm scared," I told her.

"Scared is only sacred misspelled," she answered.

I thought about that for a moment and tried to understand. Then she laughed, "It's alright to be scared, but you have to know what you're scared of. This is very unpleasant and it could get more unpleasant. You must take action."

"I know," I said rather glumly. "But I'm still scared."

"Now Christopher," she said very sweetly and gently, "You've got this big old archangel standing right behind you, and you say you're still scared. Why shame on you."

"You can see him, too?" I exclaimed.

I looked at Charlie who laughed at the expression of my face. "She trained me," was all he said.

"This is for real then?" I asked.

"As real as anything," Gladys said. "Or, as unreal as anything. All your mystics and masters have always asked what is reality and what is illusion?"

"Okay," I said, smiling as I waved her to stop. "I get it. Or, I don't get it. I mean the three of us are sitting here casually talking about an angel that probably no one else in the world can see, and that's alright. But, my two friends are being held as mindless zombies by some crazed cult leader who thinks he's the Second Coming and wants to take over the world using sound!" I paused with a sigh, "That is reality."

Grandma Gladys looked at me with a long, piercing stare. "What are you scared of boy?"

"Lots of things," I answered.

"Scared ain't nothing but sacred misspelled," Gladys repeated.

"You said that before," I told her.

"Yes, but you still don't truly understand," she replied.

"Maybe not," I admitted.

She bent over and petted the head of a large wolf dog that was asleep at her feet. I hadn't noticed the animal before.

"Everything is sacred, Christopher. Everything is an aspect of the Great Spirit. But sometimes things are twisted and that's alright. You have to have black in order to have white. It's part of the Great Spirit's plan. Do you know what I mean?"

"Yeah, I get that," I acknowledged. "Balance is part of the process of nature."

"That's right boy," she laughed. "Now what're you scared of? You scared of me?"

"Of course not," I answered.

"But you are scared of this Uncle Jude, right?"

"That's a fact, ma'am," I replied.

"Yet, Uncle Jude and I are the same," Grandma Gladys said.

"Except that you're working the light side, and he's working the dark side," I said. "He wants to control and manipulate. Do you want to do this?"

Gladys shook her head. "No, I don't Christopher. I don't need to. But Uncle Jude does. Do you know why?"

I was about to say "no", when it hit me. "Because he wants love," I said.

"That's right, Christopher. Because he wants love. And whose love does he want most of all?"

"God's love?" I asked, but I already knew it was the answer.

"God's love!" she repeated. "The love of the Great Spirit, the Creator, Wakantanka or whatever you want to call it. That love is the greatest love of all, and it is sacred. The man you call Uncle Jude is just lost and confused. That's all. He wants to find the sacred, but he's scared, scared that he can't. So instead of trusting in the natural order and finding God's love within himself, he tries to twist and manipulate things to his own workings so that people love him. Then he feels that maybe he's worthy of receiving God's love."

"Yeah," I said. "I can relate to this from a psychological or spiritual understanding of the situation. And on one level I feel sorry for Uncle Jude. But that still doesn't change the situation."

"Maybe it doesn't," Gladys said. "Maybe it does. What scares you most about Uncle Jude?"

"That I'll have to fight him," I said immediately. "He's powerful and strong, and quite frankly, I've never liked to fight."

"Just use love, child," she answered. "That's the strongest power there is."

"What?" I exclaimed.

"Use God's love, Christopher. It's the most powerful force on Mother Earth, and in the heavens as well!"

"What?" I repeated.

"Calm down boy," she said, in her soft and gentle voice. "Now, close your eyes and take a deep breath."

I did as I was told.

"Now, as you breathe in, feel God's love inside of you. Become aware of God's love as being part of everything. Everything is sacred."

I breathed in and experienced this warm glowing feeling. As I did, my heart began to tingle and my third eye began to vibrate. Suddenly, some of the memories that I had during my Lost Chord experience began to come back. I remembered the interrelationship of all things, and how the entire universe and all the different dimensionalities were connected in a web.

"Feel the energy of the Great Spirit's love," Grandma Gladys said, her voice full of wisdom and compassion. "There is nothing this love can not penetrate. Feel this love like an ocean. Know that if you can be fluid like the ocean, if you can vibrate to the different waves of this energy, then you can be part of this energy. Do not be stuck. That's what happened to your Uncle Jude. He's stuck in a place and he can't get out. To be stuck means you are fighting. It means you are scared. To be fluid allows you to change with the energy of the moment. It is like that old image of the wheat bending in the strong wind while the board that is rigid breaks. You don't have to fight anyone. All you have to do is love. Raise your vibrations when you come across Uncle Jude. He won't be able to do a thing to you."

I became aware of the multi-colored wings of my angelic friend, and was filled with an extraordinary feeling of peace and light. All the fears I had about trying to rescue Rusty and Dave, and getting back the Lost Chord, had vanished—at least for the moment.

"Everything's going to be alright," I stated, opening my eyes to the pleasant sight of Grandma Gladys and Charlie Singing Eagle looking at me.

"You bet it is," Gladys affirmed. "Just walk in the Great Spirit's path and you will be fine."

"How about if I walk in the Great Spirit's sound?" I asked, remembering what Shamael had told me about the universe being created through sound.

"Now you've got it," Gladys laughed.

"How do I do that?" I asked.

"Didn't that big angel teach you nothing?" Gladys laughed again.

"I guess he left that for you to do," I said, shrugging my shoulders.

"I guess he did," Gladys said, nodding her head. "Okay Christopher, I have teachings for you and not a lot of time. But you've had quite an education in the past few days—kind of like getting your high school diploma overnight."

"Kind of," I admitted.

"Now, it's time for a crash course in college, the College of Spiritual Knowledge," Gladys laughed. Then she turned to Charlie. "Charlie, can you scramble some eggs and make some food. This boy's going to need some nourishment. We all will."

Charlie nodded and walked over to a box to do something. I didn't follow his movements because I was once again caught in the gaze of Grandma Gladys Goodnight.

"Now, you listen good, Christopher," she began. "I'm going to teach you how to walk with the sound of the Creator."

CHAPTER 16

We left Grandma Gladys' place at eight in the morning. My advanced education degree in sonics apparently did not take as long as she had anticipated. She said I was a good student. Perhaps she was just an excellent teacher. She had come from a long line of medicine women of the Ute tradition, but like Charlie, she had decided to explore other realms of healing. She knew herbs and crystals and many other modes, but most of all, she knew sound. I was amazed to find out that when the Tibetan Monks came to Boulder, they would visit her, as would many of the Hindu Gurus and Native American Medicine Men. "My friends," she had called them. I was impressed.

Gladys lived in Rollinsville, nearly on top of Turtle Mountain, a small peak that afforded her privacy and access to Highway 119. After several miles of driving on dirt roads, we were back on paved roads. It was another half hour drive to get to Uncle Jude's Ranch in Gold Hill, but I wasn't worried. I had a deep sense of serenity. Also, I was appreciative of Charlie's companionship. I knew that beneath his quiet exterior was remarkable wisdom that would help me with the situation at the Ranch.

It started snowing on the way. Normally, I don't mind snow, especially if I'm safe and warm somewhere. But this time with the sky dark and gray, I hoped the snow wasn't an ominous foreboding of what was to occu..

My fear began to return as we turned off 72 onto the dirt road that lead to Uncle Jude's Ranch. I had been thinking of the teachings that Gladys had given me, trying to remember the chants and mantras.

"Remember that sound is sacred," she had said, "And you won't be scared."

But as we approached the electrified fence that I had driven through the night before, I realized that I was scared. The two men standing at the broken gate with rifles did not alleviate my fear.

"Looks like they didn't fix the fence," Charlie calmly observed.

"Looks like it," I said, trying to be nonchalant. It didn't work. "Charlie," I said in a panic, "Those are the two guards from yesterday. They'll recognize the car."

"Already have," Charlie said. He had been driving and now he pulled the Bronco to a complete stop as the guards raised their rifles at us. "Ear plugs in!" he said, and then turned to the backseat where the portable stereo was stashed. He switched on the play button.

The first guard, the one named Butch, pulled open the Bronco door as Charlie turned around. There was a rifle sticking into his side. The guard on my side continued pointing his weapon at my head. He was saying something, but the ear plugs prevented me from hearing what it was.

I put my hands up. Charlie did the same. The guard on my side lowered his rifle to open my door. About that time, the Lost Chord began to have an effect on Butch. His eyes became unfocused and I saw him begin to sway. My guard stuck his rifle into my ribs, but at the same cicing some changes in his companion. ply collapsed. My guard looked puzzled, d. His eyes began to glaze over, and a he was on the ground.

," I said.

"What?" Charlie asked, reaching behind him and shutting off the tape player. He removed his ear plugs, and so did I. "How long do you think these guys will stay out?" he asked.

"I don't know. They probably heard a minute of the Lost Chord. It should keep them unconscious for fifteen minutes. Maybe a half hour if we're lucky."

"We should have brought some rope to tie them," he said.

"We've had a lot on our minds," I replied.

"Well, at least let's get those rifles away from them," he stated, pulling the Winchester 30.06 from the unconscious hands of Butch. Charlie took the rifle and with one great heave, threw it thirty feet away, where it landed in the snow. He did the same with the rifle of the other guard. Then, he dragged Butch away from the Bronco. I tried the same thing with my guard, but needed help pulling his body away from the vehicle. When we were through we got back in the Bronco.

"What now?" he asked.

"Drive straight. Right before the entrance to the Ranch, there's a little service road that will take us around to the back. We won't be noticed as easily there," I said hopefully. Just then I heard a strange sound. I looked around, thinking maybe the radio button had been pushed on the stereo. Then I realized the sound was coming from outside, from the guards. "Walkie talkies!" I said. "They're trying to talk to these guards. And they're not getting any response."

Charlie nailed the Bronco. "Maybe we can get there before they figure out what's going on," he said.

No such luck. As we approached the entrance to the Ranch, there were two more guards, almost identical to Butch and his partner, standing in the middle of the snow covered dirt road with their guns pointed at us.

For a moment, I thought Charlie was going to run them over, which would have been stupid, since they could have shot us. But then he began to slow the Bronco down and stopped about 30 feet from the guards.

"Ear plugs!" he commanded. We followed the same routine as before, except this time I brought the ghetto blaster into the front seat with me and held it on my lap. It was comforting. The guards approached with their rifles pointed at us. Charlie and I raised our hands in the air as the sound of the Lost Chord filled the car.

The guards motioned for us to come out. That was okay. I opened the door, still holding the portable stereo. Then I stepped out of the Bronco. The guard on my side mouthed something I couldn't understand. He was looking at me like I was crazy, clutching the ghetto blaster to my chest. I waited for the Lost Chord to take effect and glanced round at Charlie, who was looking at me, also waiting for the sound to bring these neanderthals to the ground.

Nothing happened. Except that the guard on my side motioned for me to drop the ghetto blaster. I complied, but before I did I looked at it to make sure the tape was turning. It was. I couldn't understand it. And then I could.

"Ear plugs!" I said to myself, since I knew no one else could hear me. Either Uncle Jude had been expecting this or he was more psychic than I realized. It was probably a little of both. The guard on my side, his gun still trained on me, had picked up the portable stereo and turned it off. We were escorted at gunpoint to the main entrance of the Ranch. It was about a quarter of a mile walk and the snow was really coming down. I didn't like this at all.

Uncle Jude was standing in the front door, looking down at us. He was wearing a black, hooded robe like some medieval monk. He looked very spooky. Jude pulled back the hood of the robe. His face was gaunt and sallow.

The guard who was carrying my portable stereo held it up for Uncle Jude to see. He nodded in approval. Then he motioned for us to take the ear plugs out and hand them over. We did so.

"Mr. Shade," he called from the top of the stairs. "You are trickier than I thought. I wouldn't have given you credit for having thought of this."

"Don't", I said. "It was Charlie's idea."

"Oh," said Uncle Jude. Then he looked at Charlie. "Good idea. It might have worked on someone else."

Charlie shrugged. "It was worth a try."

Uncle Jude motioned for the two guards to remove their ear plugs. They did so.

"Are they armed?" he called out. The two guards had frisked us at the Bronco. All they found was Charlie's rattle which they returned to his back pocket, seeing no risk in a Native American percussion instrument.

"No!" one of the guards shouted back.

"Bring them in," Uncle Jude said wearily.

We walked up the steps to the entrance of the Ranch

while the guards pointed their guns at our backs. Then we were away from the snow and in the comforting arms of the lobby of the Ranch. Comforting, that is, if being captured by a messianic madman is your idea of fun.

"Mr. Shade," Uncle Jude began, "I am amazed at you, and at your friend, too. Not only did you manage to escape the chapel, but you somehow, in your audacity, have decided to return to the scene of your crime. Did you get lonely?"

"I've come to get Rusty and Dave!" I said with determination.

"What if they don't want to come?" Uncle Jude asked.

"Let me see them!" I said, trying to focus all my energy on my statement.

It didn't work. "Oh I will," said Uncle Jude. "In time, you'll join them. But for now, I have something a little more entertaining worked out for you and your friend."

"What are you talking about?" I asked.

Uncle Jude turned his back on us and began walking down the hall. The guards poked us in the back with their rifles and we began following him. "A little surprise," he said, the words drifting back to us as we walked. "I'm tired of experimenting on my people. I don't want to hurt them. But you, Mr. Shade," he stopped walking and turned towards me to emphasize his words, "have caused me a good deal of trouble. I am rather angry with you. Since your friend happens to be here as well," he pointed at Charlie and then turned back to me, "he will also take part in our little experiment."

"What are you talking about?" I asked. I was scared now and it wasn't sacred. For some reason my third eye enhancement clicked in and my fear grew worse. I was seeing these images of Charlie and me locked in a room with the Lost Chord endlessly playing. It was really scary.

"I want to find out the limits on this Lost Chord," Uncle Jude simply said. "I want to find out what happens when the human psyche is exposed to it for a prolonged period of time."

"It will kill us," I answered him. "Or drive us insane. Don't you know that?"

"I know nothing of the sort, Mr. Shade," Uncle Jude said. "You seemed to have done alright for yourself in the chapel. Let's see what happens when you are exposed to more of these sounds." He pointed to the cassette player that the guard had given him. "I take it you have the frequencies recorded on both sides?" he asked.

I didn't say anything. I wished we hadn't been so thorough in our recording the sounds of the Lost Chord. We thought it was going to help us, but that didn't seem to be the case now. Only one side had been recorded with the Lost Chord on it, but I had the feeling it would be more than adequate for Jude's purpose.

Uncle Jude examined the stereo. "Fairly cheap, but I guess it must work well enough. It immobilized my outside guards."

Both Charlie and I remained silent.

"And good!" Uncle Jude said in a sickenly sweet, almost feminine voice. "It has automatic reverse. You'll be able to listen to your favorite music until you wear the tape out." I wasn't about to tell Jude that I thought the auto reverse mechanism was broken, nor was I about to reveal that we'd recorded on only one side of the cassette. Not that it mattered. I knew what even a small dose of the Lost Chord could do. And forty five minutes was no small dose!

Suddenly his voice changed. "Come on!" he shouted in a deep and nasty tone. Then it changed again to the sweet voice. "I can't wait to see how this works!" He turned and began walking down the hall. We followed with the guards behind us.

The only vision I'd had was of Charlie and me locked in a room with the Lost Chord playing endlessly. I didn't see the cavalry. I didn't see the Indians. I didn't see anyone rescuing us. Now my third eye had closed down, or whatever you want to call it when your visions cease. All I had to accompany me was this one image of the two of us drooling ourselves to death in a locked room. It was not very comforting. I hoped it was not very accurate.

CHAPTER 17

We were led to a room somewhere in the immensity of the Ranch that was in the basement. Down one corridor, then another. Then down a flight of stairs and down another corridor. We walked for quite awhile, following Uncle Jude, no one saying a word. Finally we were at our destination.

Uncle Jude opened the door with a key from a set he was carrying and went in. We followed. We went through one room that was empty except for a wooden table and several chairs facing a glassed partition. There was a wooden door on an inside wall connecting it to another room. Using another key, Jude opened this door and stepped into the next room. Again we followed.

There was nothing in this other room. It was totally stark except for two chairs. I looked behind me to see through the large glass window. It reflected back my image—a mirror.

"Have a seat," Jude said, pointing at the two chairs. Charlie and I did as we were told.

"What is this place?" I asked. "It looks like some sort of interrogation room. Like something you'd see in a TV show."

Uncle Jude set the portable stereo unit on the floor. "Nothing of the sort," he said. "It is merely a room I use if one of my students needs special attention."

"What are you planning on doing?" I asked.

"I told you before," Jude Primer answered. "I'm going to sit in the other room. I'll watch through that two way mirror as you both experience the Lost Chord in its fullness." He pointed at the mirror which reflected nothing but our image on this side of it. Then he pointed at some speakers that were on the wall. "I can even talk with you if you like," he chuckled.

"You could use this as a recording studio," I remarked, hoping to try the connection between us as musicians again.

"I did once," Primer acknowledged. "In the early days before the real studio was up."

"And now you use it as a torture chamber," I stated.

"Hardly," Uncle Jude said, turning to leave. The two guards were in the room facing us with their rifles, now lowered, but still in their hands. I didn't feel any better.

"Wait a minute, Jude!" I called after him. He turned back to me.

"What is it?"

"Can we talk for just a minute? Please? I know you think I'm your enemy, but I'm not," I told him. Gladys had said that, like all of us, Uncle Jude was searching for love. I intended to give him that.

"Highly unlikely!" Uncle Jude snapped.

I stood up slowly with my arms open wide. Although the guards pointed their rifles again at me, I still took a step towards him. "I have nothing against you," I said. "In fact, I'm really a big fan of yours." Okay, it wasn't the truth, but I figured that this guy needed as much soothing as possible.

"That's a lie!" Primer countered.

"No, really!" I said immediately. "I really admire you." It was immediately apparent that this line of talk was not working. I knew I had to get into truth mode. "After all, we're both seeking the same thing," I gently told him.

"What's that?"

"Love of God," I said quietly.

Those words struck a resonance in Primer. He nodded his head. "Maybe," he agreed.

"We are!" I affirmed. "And I'm here to help you." I was very, very slowly making my way towards Uncle Jude, with my arms wide open. I was trying to generate as much compassion towards this man as I could. It really wasn't that difficult because I realized that we were alike, as all creatures are alike. Each of us unique and different, and yet, each a part, like an individual cell, of the great Creator.

"How?" Uncle Jude shot back. "By stealing the Lost Chord and freeing your friends?"

"I'm here to help you," I calmly said. "There's nothing to be afraid of."

"I'm not afraid of you," Primer said, his eyes growing wide. "But you should be afraid of me."

"Why?" I asked. "We're both part of the Divine aren't we? We both want to be of service to the Lord, don't we?"

Primer nodded his head. "Maybe."

I was in front of him now, still standing with my arms wide open. "Jude, I'll help you with this Lost Chord. But first, we've got to figure out what you want," I began. "I know that deep down inside you really want to help people."

"I do," he agreed.

"And that sometimes you doubt yourself."

He nodded.

"We all do," I said. "But you know, even Jesus doubted himself on the cross."

"He did," Jude affirmed.

"There's nothing to worry about," I gently said. Slowly, I raised my arms and put them around Uncle Jude. "Everything is fine. You're doing fine. You don't have to do anything to anyone. Everything is fine just the way it is."

When I put my arms around Uncle Jude, I felt this incredible love flowing out of me into him. It was genuine and it felt beautiful. I was hugging a man who was perhaps my greatest enemy, and it was wonderful.

I didn't know which particular beings were coming through me at the time. I felt like Christ, Moses, Krishna, and Buddha—all at the same time. It was unbelievable. There was this tremendous amount of energy which I can only describe as the light of love. The energy was flowing from me into Uncle Jude. I felt him receive this amazing energy, and it was extraordinary. All the anger and hatred I had felt for the man had been dissolved and was replaced by compassion. We were one being, a part of the essence of the Creator. I was truly ecstatic.

I continued hugging him and feeling the love flow out of me into him. It was a glorious experience. For a moment, I felt Jude soften and respond to this energy. For a moment, he responded and he hugged me back. I remembered Gladys' words about the power of God's love. Then, I made a mistake. I looked into Uncle Jude's eyes, and as I did, I remembered who the man was and what he was capable of. I remembered what he had done to Rusty. For a split second I felt fear. It was enough.

The next thing I knew, I felt darkness overtake Uncle Jude. I didn't know what it was, but it was frightening in its intensity. The energy was still flowing through me, but it was no longer being received. It was being repelled. Primer stiffened and pushed me away. Then, I sensed the energy stop.

"You are the spawn of Satan, come to interfere with my Divine Plan!" he shouted, pushing me away.

"No, I'm not, Jude," I said gently. "You know I'm not."

Obviously the magic spell I was weaving had been broken. I didn't know why. I didn't know how. All I knew was that Jude Primer was back to being the insane cult leader I expected him to be. I was more than a little disoriented and quite disappointed. I had thought that Grandma Gladys' magic would have been more powerful, or at least longer lasting. Perhaps I had needed more training from her. It didn't matter. We were back to square one, or perhaps worse.

I looked at Charlie and shrugged. He shrugged back. "Nice try," he said.

"Come on, Jude," I said, ready to try using the power of love once more. It had almost worked—maybe a second exposure to this energy would be able to dispel the darkness in Primer.

Uncle Jude looked at the guards and pointed at his ear. The two men slipped on ear plugs one at a time. One would put his rifle down and put in the ear plugs. Then the other. It looked like they had rehearsed it. I was almost impressed. Neither one of them allowed Charlie or me the opportunity to escape past them—not that we had the inclination to do so. Well, actually, I did consider the possibility, but since it did not present itself, I merely marveled at the guards' ear plug precision.

"You can't do this, Jude," I said sternly.

"Why not?" he asked.

"We'll be missed in Boulder," I replied.

"I'm not going to kill you," Primer responded.

"You don't know what overexposure to the Lost Chord will do!" I protested.

"It probably won't kill you," he said. "I'll be interested in seeing what it does, though. It will let me know about the human tolerance for the Lost Chord."

"Jude, we're here to help you!"

Uncle Jude pointed at the chair next to Charlie. "Sit down, Mr. Shade, and don't get up. I'm going to put your little tape recorder on. If you try to turn it off, I will have my guards stop you."

"What are they going to do? Shoot me if I press the stop button?" I said sarcastically.

"Only if they have to," Uncle Jude said seriously.

"Better sit down, Christopher," Charlie said. "They probably won't put a bullet in you, but if you've ever been hit by a rifle butt, you'd probably rather not repeat the experience."

"But I haven't been Charlie," I said.

"Sit down, Mr. Shade," Uncle Jude said. "I am losing my patience."

"I think you lost that with your sanity!" I said, blasting him with a wave of negativity. So much for my attempt to beam love at him. I needed more training.

Uncle Jude motioned to one of the bear-like guards who took a step towards me. I held up my hands and sat in the chair. "Okay," I said. "But this is the last time I play musical chairs with you."

Charlie looked at me and shook his head. He mouthed the word, "What?" to me. Obviously my sense of humor had its ups and downs.

Uncle Jude took out a pair of ear plugs which he played with while he talked. "I'll be in the next room watching. Don't try any funny stuff. If you turn off the recorder, we'll just have to tie you up and do it the hard way. Okay?"

"I just don't get you, Jude," I said. "There's no need to do this."

"Yes there is!" Jude Primer said. Then he put the ear plugs in his ears, and hit the play button on the tape recorder.

CHAPTER 18

What you are probably expecting now is that once again I will have an encounter with the Angel of Sound while the Lost Chord is jamming in my ears. The angel will eventually give me the strength to return to my body despite the extraordinary wonderment of going through the dimensional gateway. This might have happened. I truly believe it might have happened. I truly expected it to happen, that is, if Grandma Gladys' sonic recipe didn't work. But it did.

What really happened is this: from the moment Uncle Jude hit the play button on the cassette player, both Charlie and I began quietly chanting a mantra Gladys had given us. Actually, she'd given us half a dozen to work with in case the first wasn't effective. That, of course, is supposing that we'd still be in any shape to do anything if the first mantra wasn't effective. But it was.

Now, I have to tell you that while I am no great authority on mantras, this was definitely not one I'd ever heard. It sounded very Native American, but I couldn't be sure. Since I was sworn to secrecy on this one, I can not accurately repeat it. But, I have to admit that I had my doubts about its effectiveness. It did sound a bit like, "I can't find my laundry list, itchy man of mine." Though of course that wasn't it. And, as I've already told you, it was an effective antidote to the Lost Chord.

Mantras, as I've said, are words of power that are found in different cultures. Probably the most famous mantras are the ones found in the Hindu and the Tibetan traditions. They are also found in practically every tradition and culture on the earth. Anytime that someone sits, and vocally, or silently repeats the name of God, they are actually intoning a mantra. Sitting around chanting "Jesus", "Jehovah", "Allah", or "Hallelujah" is really mantric chanting. So is toning "Om" for a long period of time. "Om" has many translations, but it is commonly understood to mean "peace". At any one time there are probably thousands of people throughout the planet who are chanting "Om", which makes it a very powerful mantra, since you can tap into the energy field of all those people who are making this particular sound.

Mantras can get very complicated and very specific. In the Hindu and Tibetan traditions there are many levels of mantras. Some of them are very simple, like chanting the name of a deity. The idea is that if one chants this mantra for long enough (usually these traditions believe that 108 times is the minimum energy required), you actually begin to vibrate to the energy of the being whose name you are chanting and become one with that being. I understand that this is a very powerful practice. If you become one with a deity, it seems that your entire vibrational level changes—at least momentarily—and you can supposedly achieve miraculous experiences, from physical healing to communication with higher levels of consciousness.

I wondered what it would be like to chant "Shamael" for awhile. Would that, without the aid of the Lost Chord, bring me in communication with the Angel of Sound? I contemplated trying that as soon as we were able to get our of the present situation.

Grandma Gladys had told me that a secret to make the chanting of sacred mantras even more effective, was to couple the vocalization, or the actual chanting of the mantra, with a specific visualization pertaining to the mantra. Shamael had given me similar information. It must have really been important!

Gladys had said that in Tibet, where the monks will chant specific mantras for hours, they have these very advanced visualizations called "Mandalas". These visualizations may have over a hundred different specific deities in particular places. There are particular planes of consciousness that the monks create through their thoughts. Then, coupled with the chanting of the mantras, which alters their physical body, brain waves, and energy fields, the monks can actually go into the different mandalas they have created and have visitations from the beings they are invoking.

The visualization that Gladys had given me for the mantra I was chanting was very simple. It just involved my imagining a cord of energy going from the base of my spine into the earth. And also beams of energy going from the bottom of my feet into the earth. The mantra was intoned in the deepest voice that I could make; it did not have to be a loud voice—I was to feel the sound resonating at the base of my spine while I felt that cord going deep into the earth. She said it was the most powerful grounding mantra she knew and that it should be effective in keeping the Lost Chord from pulling me out of my body. The other mantras she had given me were to be used in case the first one wasn't effective. They all had specific purposes. One was a protection mantra. Another was an invisibility mantra. Another was to be used in case I was taken out of my body. I was to chant it no matter where I was taken, in order to return to my body. But, as I said, it wasn't necessary. Her grounding mantra worked well.

Gladys had said that while she believed the Lost Chord was extremely powerful, she didn't think that it would be more powerful than an individual who was using a specific mantra with a visualization and focused intention. I had tried to explain to her how utterly mind shattering my experience with the Lost Chord had been. She had listened with great attention, but then shook her head.

"No, boy," she'd commented. "I hear what you're telling me, but it just doesn't make sense. You've never experienced the power of your own self-created sounds. I just don't think anything can compare with making your own sounds. Don't you think the spirits can differentiate between an electronically created frequency that's calling them and the energy of the human spirit?"

"I guess," I had said. I really didn't know. Or at least I wasn't sure. That is, until Charlie and I began to chant the grounding mantra she had given us. Actually, I wasn't sure that Charlie and I were using the same mantra. I just assumed it. Later on Charlie confirmed it. It didn't matter though. As soon as we started chanting that mantra, the Lost Chord didn't have much of an effect. Oh, I felt a little bit light headed, but it was nothing—not nearly as powerful as the millisecond bursts of the Lost Chord which I had experienced in the Chapel the day before. I was basically clear headed and fully conscious. And, more than a little angry at Uncle Jude. I had tried, with great sincerity, to use the power of love to change his attitude, but it hadn't worked. I guessed that it probably would have taken a little longer to affect his hardened heart than I had initially presumed. That moment of fear I had experienced might have been all that was necessary for the dark forces to regain control of Uncle Jude. I kept telling myself that I simply needed more training than I had received. Unfortunately, I just did not have the time to practice at transforming Jude. Rather, it was he who had the time and was trying to transform Charlie and me via the Lost Chord.

Charlie and I sat there quietly intoning this mantra to ourselves while the white noise of the Lost Chord blared out of the stereo speakers. After the panic of being exposed to the Lost Chord and not loosing consciousness had left me, and the other fears had subsided, I looked into the mirror that was really a one way window and grinned my biggest smile at Uncle Jude. I knew he'd be furious.

I concentrated on the mantra and continued repeating it, smiling at the mirror. Still chanting the mantra, I pointed at the stereo system on the floor and shrugged my shoulders. I could sense Uncle Jude's fury from the next room.

Suddenly, the door burst open. There was Jude Primer looking at us in disbelief. Charlie and I remained sitting, both of us now grinning. We could see the two guards in the hallway, but they did not enter the room.

Primer looked at us, then bent down and looked at the portable stereo to see if it was running. It was. Charlie and I continued grinning and chanting our mantra. Then Jude Primer did something that was a mistake. He pulled out his ear plugs.

The mantra grew louder in my head as I chanted it. I watched Jude's eyes glaze over. Then, he began to sway back and forth and finally, he collapsed on the ground. That was when Charlie and I made our break for the door.

The two guards watched as Uncle Jude fell to the floor. I knew they were wearing ear plugs and wouldn't fall for the same thing, if you'll pardon my pun.

Charlie hit the first guard with his body, almost before I was out of my chair. Could he move fast! By the time I was out in the hallway, all I saw was a blur of hands as the second guard pitched backwards, hit the wall and slide down unconscious onto the floor.

Then, I was racing after Charlie, following him down the hall. "We've got to move quickly," he said.

"Where'd you learn those moves?" I asked.

"Special Forces," he said. "Years ago in Vietnam. I hate to use violence, but it's something you don't forget."

"Pretty effective," I quipped, though I don't think he heard me.

We were running through the halls now and had found the staircase that led up to the first floor. Charlie paused for a moment, giving me time to catch up with him. "Where are we going?" I panted.

"We've got to get out of here," Charlie said rather calmly. He was hardly winded at all. "Those guards," he pointed toward the area we had just run from, "will be after us soon."

"How long will they be out?" I asked.

"It's hard to say," he said. As if on cue, we heard some movement from down the hall and both of us ran up the stairs.

At the top of the stairs Charlie started for the front entrance of the Ranch. "Come on," he said. "We've got to get out of here."

"We can't leave without finding Rusty and Dave," I told him, grabbing his arm and pulling him in the direction of the chapel.

"We've got to leave now, Christopher," Charlie said, pulling away from me and grabbing me by both arms. He looked in my eyes and shook me. "This is a very serious situation. Those guards have guns. We don't. Come on now."

I returned Charlie Singing Eagles look with one of deep calm and knowing. "Trust me!" I said.

Charlie sighed and let go of me.

"Okay," I said, beginning to walk quickly towards the back entrance of the Ranch. Charlie joined me as we headed to the door that led to the chapel. I could hear noises from behind us as we ran to the door.

"To the chapel!" I shouted. "We've got to rescue Dave and Rusty!"

We were at the door that led to the walkway when the first bullet whizzed by me, striking the glass door, shattering it. There was no need for me to open the door at that point. I stepped through the glass, running for the door of the chapel. Another bullet went by.

"Are you chanting your protection mantra?" I asked, as I silently began to repeat the mantra that Gladys had given me. I hoped I was doing it right. I prayed that it worked.

"I've been doing it for the last five minutes" he admitted.

"They won't fire at us in the chapel," I shouted to Charlie.

"Let's hope!" he said.

I couldn't believe that the guards were actually shooting at us. The idea was somewhat terrifying, and at the same time exciting. A third shot rang out and a bullet tore by me, missing my head by an inch. I didn't know if the protection mantra was working, but that last shot was much to close for comfort. The adrenaline was pumping as I hit the door to the chapel, with Charlie right behind me.

I took a step back as Charlie reached ahead of me and opened the door. I went in first and turned my head to check our pursuers. They were now at the back door to the Ranch, about to enter the walkway to the chapel. Then Charlie and I were in. I slammed the door behind us. We both had the same idea—lock the door behind us! It didn't take any great thinking to realize that this was our only hope. Whether or not the guards were willing to use their rifles in the chapel was another story. If they couldn't get into the chapel, it would be a lot easier for us.

There were two doors that led into the chapel. One that led from the walkway, and one that I had used the day before to get outside when I was in the chapel. Both had two different locks on them. One lock could be opened with a key. The other lock, however, had a bolt on it. We locked the doors using both types of locks, hoping that even if the guards had keys, they wouldn't be able to break down the door. At least not immediately.

I couldn't see the guards from outside, but I could hear them. They banged on the first door several times. Both of them were apparently hitting the door with all their weight. But the doors were well constructed and the guards didn't seem to be able to break through. The fact that Charlie was bracing his weight against the door helped as well. Then, the pounding stopped.

I turned to Charlie. "They can't get in!" I said proudly. "See, trust me. We're okay."

Charlie shook his head and sighed deeply. "Christopher," he said, "This is the worst." He had a disgusted look on his face as he worked his jaw, assessing the situation.

I looked at him, not understanding. "What do you mean Charlie?" I asked. "We're finally safe."

Charlie pointed at one of the windows. We could see the guards outside.

"I still don't think they'll shoot at us in here," I said. "Too many people."

"Probably not," Charlie said. "You're probably right. But you see, there is one thing."

"What's that?" I asked.

"There's one thing you haven't figured out yet. But I imagine you'll figure it out sooner or later," he said, an amused smile on his face. "But maybe I should tell you."

"What's that?" I repeated again.

"They can't get in, but we can't get out, my friend." He looked at me, still smiling as the truth of the situation began to sink in. "We're trapped."

CHAPTER 19

Okay, so we were trapped. Maybe there were two guards with rifles waiting outside for us. So what? I was Christopher Shade, Spiritual Detective, and I'd been in worse spots. Like the time that club owner refused to pay us and I had to hire a lawyer to get our money. Like the time that drug dealer confused me with one of his customers and I had to hide out at a friend's for a week. Like the time one of my past girlfriends refused to pay for her portion of dinner at a restaurant. Yeah, I'd been in tougher spots. But I couldn't think when.

What can I say? I'm a pretty passive person. And, although I admit to having taken some karate training in my youth, I avoid violence like the plague. I would rather run than fight when in a tough situation. I was really good at running, and that's just what I had done. I'd run into the chapel where two excuses for human beings were waiting to recapture us, or shoot us. I don't think they cared which. Still, for some reason, I felt very calm. Then, as I turned around from the door and looked at the inside of the chapel I realized why.

"The Lost Chord," I said. "Jude still has it playing". Instantly, I began to silently recite the grounding mantra. I knew that Charlie was doing the same. It probably didn't have the same effect as chanting it aloud, but then Uncle Jude wasn't using the complete

Lost Chord in the chapel, only millisecond bursts of it. As the mantra began resonating within me, my calmness and serenity were replaced by a sense of loathing.

"Oh my God!" I gasped, as I looked around. Actually, there was nothing really unusual about what I saw. In fact, it looked exactly the same as when I had left it the day before. Everyone was sitting in exactly the same positions. The smell of urine and feces drifted into my nostrils. No one had noticed the commotion that had been created when Charlie and I had slammed into the place.

"They're like zombies!" I whispered.

"We've got to cut the sound," Charlie simply said. I nodded and looked around. There was a series of speakers, six to be exact, that surrounded the inside of the dome. They were mounted on the wall eight feet above the floor.

"There are our culprits," I pointed to to speakers.

Charlie nodded. "Christopher, do you think there's a main source that we can deactivate?"

I looked around trying to find some central wiring point which connected all the speakers. The music that was softly playing from the speakers was the same music I'd heard when I'd been in the chapel before. Obviously, Uncle Jude had only experimented with one of his recordings using the Lost Chord. While I was not totally familiar with Jude Primer's musical works, this one was a sickeningly sweet, spiritual series of ballads called, "Thy Will Be Done". I think it had been released sometime in the 80's, and was Uncle Jude's opus to "The Lord's Prayer". It had been a nice idea, but a huge flop, hitting the cut out bins almost immediately after it was released. I guessed that either Uncle Jude had a special fondness for this recording, or it had been the first music he'd grabbed for his experiments.

I saw a junction box that was about two feet to the left of the main door. "I think that's it!" I said, nudging Charlie in the side with my elbow.

Charlie nodded again. "Where are your friends?" he asked.

I pointed to Rusty and Dave. They were sitting in the same place I had left them, in an outer circle on the floor. I hadn't tried to go to them yet. I didn't know what I might find. I knew that after we dismantled the sound system this would be my next step.

"Go and check on them," Charlie said.

"Maybe we should wait until we take care of the sound," I suggested.

"No!" Charlie said firmly. "Do it now."

I very stealthfully walked up to where Rusty and Dave were sitting. They had been there for almost 24 hours. My heart sank as I approached. Rusty still looked as beautiful as always, but I was afraid she'd give me the same "Get away!" statement she had the day before when I had tried to get her to leave.

There was a bathroom in the chapel, and apparently some of the people trapped by the sonics had somehow had the inner guidance to use the toilets despite their somnambulant state. As I neared Rusty and Dave, it seemed they had been among those who had been guided, and I was quite glad.

Here's a little aside; the whole "Shade" bit began because of my eyes. I have poor eyesight and wear photo gray tinted lens to disguise the thickness of my glasses. It's not that I'm really into wearing dark glasses all the time, but rather I do it for my image. My eyes are so bad, I can't even wear contact lenses. So, the tinted photo grays work. They're real dark in the sunlight and give the impression of sunglasses even in the dim light of a nightclub. It helps with my rock n' roll persona; Shade, the man with dark glasses, dark hair, and dark clothes. It's all illusion.

Although my sense of sight is hopeless, my sense of hearing and my sense of smell are extremely sensitive. That was why, once I tuned into the scents of the chapel, it was all I could do to keep from getting sick. It was also why I was quite grateful that Rusty and Dave had used the bathroom.

I sat down behind Rusty and gently touched her on the shoulder. She looked at me. Her eyes were glazed and she looked as zombiefied as everyone else. As she looked at me, I saw a tear form. "Shade," she mumbled, "Please help me!" Then the blankness appeared back in her expression and she turned away from me.

"Don't worry Rusty," I said. "I will." I hoped she had heard me.

I moved to Dave and did the same thing, putting my hand on his shoulder. There was no response. I shook him gently for about half a minute. Finally, he turned. He looked so stoned. "What, man?" was all he said. Then he turned away from me. Obviously, prolonged exposure to the Lost Chord affected different people differently.

I was hoping that with a little help, Rusty could break the spell of the Chord. I began to chant the grounding mantra out loud in her ears. First the left ear, then the right ear. I chanted for about a minute. Suddenly, Rusty shuddered. "Oh my God!" she said as she looked at me. "What's been happening? How long have I been here?"

"About a day, Rusty," I told her. "I was able to leave, but you wouldn't go. Are you ready to join me now?"

"Shade, you don't know," she began. Then I think the effects of the Lost Chord began to hit her again. "Oh God," she said, a look of pain on her face. "It's happening again. I can't leave. I'm stuck here."

I realized that I could sit there and continuously chant the grounding mantra for her and Dave, and it would probably bring them both back to some semblance of consciousness. But, it still didn't resolve the situation. I looked through one of the windows and saw one of the guards standing outside, waiting for us, rifle in hand. It was snowing hard now, and he was covered with a layer of white. I wondered if he was cold and miserable. I hoped so. A plan was slowly beginning to form in my brain.

"I'll be back," I said to Rusty. "Don't worry. It'll all be alright."

I got up and turned to Charlie, who was silently sitting behind me. "We've got to dismantle the sound system!" I said.

Charlie was up immediately from his sitting position. He moved in one fluid wave. It was remarkable to see. It took me a couple of seconds to use my hands to help lift myself up and straighten out. Then I joined Charlie at the junction box. It was the place where all the wiring for the speakers connected. "You don't happen to have a knife to cut these wires do you?" I asked Charlie, knowing he didn't.

"We don't need no stinkin' knife," Charlie said with a sly grin. He reached up and with one mighty pull, tore all the wiring out of the wall, breaking the electrical connection. Uncle Jude's voice and music immediately died in the chapel. I don't know what I expected at that moment, but nothing happened.

"The grounding chant!" I said to Charlie in a panic.

Charlie held up a hand, motioning for me to stop. He reached into his back pocket and pulled out the rattle he had been carrying. I had forgotten about it.

"This is good for breaking fields," he said. "A lot of them are still caught in the field, even though the music has died."

Grandma Gladys had told me about sonic fields, about how sound can create fields of energy that, while invisible, can be as strong as physical matter that you see. The Lost Chord created such a field. In 5 minutes, the Chord created a field that was so powerful it took more than an hour to dissipate. I guessed that after being held for more than 24 hours in the field of Uncle Jude's version of the Lost Chord, with its millisecond bursts of sonic energy, most of the people in the chapel needed a lot more time to return to normal. Time, however, was something we did not have.

"Clap your hands!" Charlie shouted as he began shaking the rattle and singing the grounding chant in a loud, clear voice. I joined him. Due to the acoustics of the geodesic dome, our voices filled the chapel, echoing and reverberating. It really sounded neat.

Gladys had told me that one of the easiest ways of breaking up fields was using harsh, percussive sounds. She said that in ancient China, the reason that fireworks had been invented was to scare away evil demons and break their field. Drums and rattles also had this ability. So did clapping. She said it was a pity that Western audiences would applaud after a musical performance, since this destroyed the field that had been created by the music.

I clapped along with Charlie's rattle. We continued to chant the grounding mantra together. In less than a minute, I began to notice an effect. People began to break out of the daze they were in and look around. We moved close to Rusty and Dave who were staring at us.

I stopped clapping for a moment and motioned for the two of them to join us. Then, I went back to clapping, watching as Rusty and Dave attempted to move. They were obviously quite stiff from their prolonged sitting and it took them a few minutes to finally rise. Meanwhile, as Charlie and I continued our chanting, the field of Uncle Jude's music coupled with the Lost Chord was almost totally dissipated. Others in the chapel were beginning to stretch and move, although I don't think anyone else had figured out what had happened to them.

I cast a glance outside and saw the guard put his hand above his forehead in an attempt to get a better view of what was happening inside the chapel. Thirty men and women in the chapel were now starting to get up and look around, a confused expression on their faces. Rusty and Dave were now standing, having joined Charlie and me as we chanted. "Clap!" was all I said. Rusty was the first to help create more percussive sounds. Then Dave finally got it together. I knew neither one of them understood what was going on, but it didn't matter. Their sounds helped.

I told you that I'd had the vague meanderings of a plan forming in my head. It wasn't really so much a plan, as an image. It was from *Torn Curtain*, a movie that starred Paul Newman. I couldn't recall most of the movie but I could remember this one scene when Paul and his lady friend, played by Julie Andrews, are trapped in a crowded movie theater by the bad guys. Suddenly, Paul begins to yell "Fire!" and they are able to escape. At the time I saw it, I thought it was a pretty ingenious way of exiting a trap. Now, I was ready to try it myself and see if it really worked.

"Fire!" I shouted at the top of my lungs. "Fire! Fire! Fire!"

Charlie stopped chanting and looked at me in puzzlement. Then, he understood. "Fire!" he began to shout.

In a moment, the serenity that had filled the chapel was now replaced by panic. It wasn't very nice, but it was all I had hoped. You would be amazed at the chaos and pandemonium that can arise from people who have been awakened from a somnambulant, semi-spiritual condition to find themselves in a life threatening situation. You might think that with all the training they had, these people would calmly walk through the doors. But they didn't.

In a matter of moments, the thirty people who were in the chapel were screaming and running with arms flailing. They were pushing each other out of the way in an attempt at being next out of the chapel. I had seen little children in a fire drill behave more appropriately, but I suppose I was to blame. A couple of minutes before, most of the people in the chapel had been having some sort of deeply serene, perhaps spiritual experience. Now, visions of flaming hell were probably burning in their brains. I'm sure it wasn't a very pleasant experience. And, of course, Charlie and I continued yelling, "Fire!" to make sure the situation did not change.

Half the people exited out the door that led back to the Ranch. The other half stampeded out the door that lead to the outside. Rusty, Dave, Charlie and I joined those who went out the door to the outside. We were able to push so that we were in the middle of the line that poured out the door.

I don't know what the guard standing in the snow was thinking when he began to see the crowd of people streaming out the door. He had put his rifle down and was standing with his mouth open. Snow had fallen on him and he looked like a befuddled snowman. At another time, it might have been quite amusing, but not now. Men and women moved past him, screaming. Even if he had spotted us in the line of people running through the door, I don't know what he could have done. I didn't know what the other guard at the other door was doing either. Probably the same thing. It was difficult to try and capture or shoot someone when you're involved in chaos.

As I passed the guard, he recognized me. I grabbed his rifle. He was much bigger than me, and I suppose in a contest of brute force he would have been able to pull his rifle back. Of course, I could have tried to use some of the karate moves I had been trained in, but it wasn't necessary.

Charlie smashed the guard in the solar plexus with his elbow. The guard doubled over. I saw Singing Eagle's hands move in a blur, and I knew they connected with the guard's head, although I couldn't be sure where. I did see the bear-like guard fall backward into the snow. He was out cold, a trickle of blood coming from his nose.

"Is he dead?" I asked.

"Doubtful," Charlie said. People were still stampeding past us. Some disoriented people had trampled the guard on the ground. I was pretty sure he hadn't felt a thing.

"Come on," Charlie said, motioning for us to follow

him. I could tell that Rusty and Dave were very weak, the result of listening to the Lost Chord for 24 hours without food.

"They need help," I said. Charlie went over to Dave, putting his arms around his shoulder for support. I did the same for Rusty. It was the closest I'd ever been to her, and I briefly breathed in her energy. Then I remembered where I was and focused on the situation.

Charlie was leading us away from the Ranch. "Where are we going?" I asked.

"Up there!" Charlie said, pointing ahead of us.

"You're kidding," I answered. I had noticed the formidable mountain behind the Ranch when I had escaped the chapel the day before. At the time, due to the darkness, all I sensed was an ominous feeling since it was impossible to scope the immensity of the mountain. Now, in the day, despite the intense snow, I peered up. Some might call it a foothill. Others might call it a mountain. From where I stood, it looked at least a few thousand feet to the top.

I'm sure that in the summer, it would have been a beautiful walk to the top of this peak—not too steep and full of all sorts of wildflowers. In the snow, however, with two weakened comrades, it seemed impossible to ascend.

Charlie did not stop as we began to approach the base of the mountain, which was marked by a field of pine trees. He kept on going, motioning for us to follow him.

"You're kidding," I repeated. "Rusty and Dave can barely walk."

"Then we'll have to carry them," Charlie said.

"I'm okay, Shade," Dave said, panting. "At least this

is better than spending the rest of my life in the chapel listening to that disgusting music of Uncle Jude. He is the worst!"

"Christopher," Rusty began, "It was awful. After awhile I began to understand what was happening, and how we were trapped there. But, I had no will to fight." She looked at me with her remarkable green eyes. "How did you fight it?"

"Later," I said, trying to follow Charlie. "Charlie!" I screamed in anger. "Why the hell are we going up this mountain?"

Suddenly, a shot rang out and I knew the answer. A moment later all four of us were hidden by pine trees. We were safe, at least temporarily. But, as we continued making our way up, the snow was getting deeper and deeper, and it was getting colder and colder. I didn't know how Rusty and Dave were doing. Somehow, they had remembered to grab their jackets when they left the chapel. Charlie and I had never had time to remove our winter outer layers. Still, what we were wearing was never meant to be a barrier against the elements we were facing.

Everyone except for Charlie was huffing and puffing as we attempted to ascend the mountain. After all we'd been through, this was the last straw. I knew we could not take it. Yet, I also knew that at least one, and probably two or more men with rifles were following us. I also knew they would shoot to kill. I was pretty sure at that point in time and space, that I was going to die.

So, I stopped for a moment, looked Rusty in the eyes and said, "Rusty, I love you." Then I kissed her full on the mouth, holding her tightly and feeling her body against mine. I suppose you could say it was not exactly appropriate timing, but when you're sure you're going to die, it's hard to find moments that are appropriate.

We must have held each other for a minute, maybe two minutes. Despite the cold and the snow and the fatigue and everything else, I've got to tell you that those may have been two of the happiest minutes of my life. It wasn't sexual. it wasn't even sensual. It was momentarily, being embraced by a feeling of total love—a man and a woman uniting as one. Brief as the experience was, it allowed me to understand new possibilities of relationship, of being with another who could receive love and return love. It was wonderful.

Rusty didn't say anything to me. She didn't have too. Maybe it was because I had attempted to rescue her, or maybe she had liked me all along but had been too put off by my cocky behavior. Whatever the reason, as Rusty kissed and hugged me back, I knew that my feelings for her were being reciprocated. I was in heaven. Or at least heaven on earth.

"Come on, Christopher! You can save that for later!" Charlie shouted. The spell was broken. I was back in the cold and the snow and the tiredness. And again, I knew I was going to die.

CHAPTER 20

Was it love or confusion? Frankly, I didn't know and more frankly, I didn't care. I guess I'd had what might be called a crush on Rusty Fox ever since I had first been introduced to her by Dave. Unfortunately, at that point in time and space, I couldn't differentiate very well between sexual infatuation and what might be called a deep bonding of the heart.

I didn't know Rusty well. She had never really given me the opportunity to get to know her. I'd been impressed by her mind and her musical ability, and as I've pointed out before, the way she looked. Of course, you could point out that the conditions under which we had our first kiss were, to say the least, rather stressful. To tell you the truth, probably the last thing I consciously had on my mind as we headed up that mountain was to stop, confess my feelings to Rusty, and to plant a wet one on her. To be more truthful, perhaps it was indeed confusion that caused me to act in that manner. Or, maybe it was my spirit guides, or Shamael, or whatever alternate entity or energy form you want to name that took over for me.

Regardless, I will never forget that kiss. There was electricity and more that passed between Rusty and me. I'd heard about tantra, which is a way in which a man and a woman could make love from a spiritual aspect:

the man becomes the embodiment of the divine masculine god and the woman becomes the embodiment of the divine feminine. I knew at that moment, that if given the opportunity, Rusty and I could create miraculous energetics together. Then, Charlie shouted at me and it was over. I was back at the bottom of the mountain in a blizzard, heading God knows where, for God knows what purpose, except to avoid being shot, which to be truthful, was a pretty good reason to do anything.

It was a slow trek going up the mountain. I saw Charlie up ahead pulling Dave, who looked a bit like a ragged puppet being pulled by a giant. I did my best to gently help Rusty along. She was in better shape than I thought, despite her day long episode with the Lost Chord. Who knows? Maybe regardless of the lack of food and movement, she had somehow been energized by the long meditational experience.

The snow kept getting deeper and deeper. I wish we'd had snowshoes, or at least skies—Not that I'm a skier or know very much about the sport. I am, in fact, probably the only human living in the Boulder area who doesn't ski. I've just never liked it. Yes, I've tried it on occasion. I was just never very good at it. I remember once going skiing with a friend who was an expert skier, and also a metaphysical wizard. He had promised that he would turn skiing into a spiritual experience for me. First, he made me do some practice runs by myself. Then, he came to me and shook his head in amusement. "Shade, my dear friend," he said with a smile, "You must get over your fear. It was impossible for you to go straight towards that tree without you actually turning your skis to do so."

I thanked my friend, took off my skis, and realized that different people enjoyed different things. For me, skiing was not one of those things. There was nothing wrong with that. I like the beach and the ocean. I'm not a surfer, but I sure can relax on a sailboat in the middle of the deep blue sea. What I'm doing in the land of snow and skiing is another story. I think I told you it had to do with following a woman from Boston to Boulder.

Now, there I was again stuck in the middle of the cold and the white and it was essentially because of a woman. Well, I mean after all, Rusty did start the whole thing. If she had not created the Lost Chord in the first place, it never would have been stolen and we never would have been captured trying to retrieve it, and now I wouldn't be in the process of trying to save her or myself.

"Try to walk gently," Charlie called back to us as the snow became deeper and deeper. I was doing my best but there were places where the snow was more than three feet deep, and times when my full weight caused it to collapse, and I would sink in the snow up to my waist. We had gone about three hundred yards since my memorable kiss with Rusty when I realized that Charlie had stopped. It had taken ten or fifteen minutes to go that far, and I could see that Charlie was concerned. We could hear the sound of shouts and curses from below us. The guards were close and moving much faster than we were. They must have taken the time to put on snow shoes before they came after us.

Rusty and I made it to Charlie and Dave. Charlie was sitting on the snow cross-legged. "Sit down," he said.

I motioned to the sounds below us.

"Sit down," he repeated. "If we don't do something quickly, they'll catch up. Another minute or two is not going to matter." Rusty, Dave and I sat down.

"What?" I asked.

"Christopher," Charlie began, "I know this snow is deep and difficult to walk on, but it's almost as though you are visualizing the fact that you're too heavy for the snow."

I snorted. "I am," I laughed.

Charlie looked at me sternly. "Stop it," he said. "Visualize yourself light as a feather. You too, Miss," he told Rusty. "And you, too," Charlie said, turning to Dave. All three of us nodded.

"Do you remember the levitation mantra that Gladys gave you?" Charlie asked me.

"I think so," I said. I repeated what I thought that mantra was.

"That's right," Charlie said. "Repeat it again."

I did so.

"Now all three of you repeat it," Charlie instructed us.

We did so.

"Now, I want all three of you to be chanting that mantra as we go up the mountain," Charlie continued. "I want you to visualize that all three of you are light as feathers and that the snow can support your weight. I don't think any of you are going to start floating away. This mantra is much too complex for that, requiring extreme discipline to achieve levitation. I've never done it myself. But I have noticed that even casual repetition of the mantra does seem to affect gravitational fields."

"Really?" Dave said in amazement.

"Really," Charlie answered in sincerity, nodding his head. "Christopher here has had some private instruction in sound and he's seen what some of these mantras can do."

"It's true," I said.

"But, he also seems to have some resistance to the snow," Charlie countered.

"It's true," I repeated.

"So, all three of you are in the same situation. But you've got to try it, and you've got to believe. As my teacher told Christopher, the thing about mantras and chants is not just the words alone. They work, but not as effectively as when they're coupled with the imaging or visualization. Do you understand?"

Rusty, Dave and I nodded our heads in agreement. Charlie stood up. He was a big man, much bigger than me. But the snow had not collapsed under him. It was like he was weightless. "Okay now," he said to us, "Let me hear that mantra."

Rusty, Dave and I began chanting the mantra aloud.

"Are you visualizing yourself light as feathers?" Charlie asked.

The three of us nodded.

Charlie stretched out a hand and pulled Rusty up. Then he pulled Dave up, and finally me. We continued chanting the mantra. Charlie began moving up the mountain. Rusty, Dave and I followed.

It was amazing! I am not kidding. Not once did the snow falter under any of our footsteps. We chanted and visualized and walked and it was truly amazing. It was as if we were light as feathers. It was as if the snow was strong enough to support our weight. Suddenly, we were making a most rapid ascent up this mountain.

"I can't believe this!" I shouted.

"Keep your voice down," Charlie hissed back. "It'll give away our position and could start an avalanche."

"Avalanche?" I repeated. Crash. I was back, buried

waist deep in the snow.

"Keep chanting the mantra and visualizing," Charlie repeated in a soft, but stern voice. Rusty and Dave gave me a hand out of the snow. Together, the three of us chanted the levitation mantra as we followed Charlie Singing Eagle up the mountain.

A word about the levitation mantra or rather a question: did it work? I can only report to you that after Charlie gave us his pep talk, we made it to the top of the mountain in what seemed like a few minutes. It was probably more like half an hour, but time really speeds up when you're experiencing supernatural abilities.

Maybe it was purely mind over matter—I don't know. Once, some years ago, I tried fire walking. I was really scared at the time, but did it with a lady friend of mine. When she went across the burning coals, I knew I had to do it. So, I repeated the mantra I was given at the time, "Cool moss! Cool moss!" and visualized that I was stepping on exactly that. In truth, it didn't hurt a bit. I was amazed and elated when I ended up on the other side of the coals.

Then I saw my lady friend Carol, who was soaking her foot. I asked her what happened. She told me that for one second, the "Cool moss!" mantra disappeared from her mind and she thought, "I can't be doing this!". It was during this time that she received a blister, which covered the bottom of her foot. So, mind over matter, using a mantra or just working on visualization—I don't know what was responsible for giving Rusty, Dave and me the ability to fly up the mountain with Charlie. But we did it. And then we were on top. The same amazement and elation I had felt after walking over hot coals overcame me. For about one minute, I breathed in the thin air and marveled at the seemingly miraculous experience that had just occurred. Then another reality set in.

It was freezing cold. The snow was falling hard. The wind was whipping our faces. Suddenly, I looked at Charlie and asked, "What are we doing here?"

Charlie looked at me. I think the same thought had occurred to him now that we had arrived at our destination. "It seemed like a good idea at the time," were his words of wisdom.

"Oh great!" I said with more than a little of a defeated attitude. "We'd have been better off running back into the Ranch with the others."

"I don't think so," Charlie replied. "At least we're alive and free," he said softly.

"And freezing to death with a bunch of armed loonies about to use us for target practice," I answered, pointing to four figures I saw below.

We were above tree line. Maybe a thousand feet higher. The figures below us looked like ants, trudging their way up the mountain. I was pretty sure they couldn't see us, but that didn't make matters any better.

"Maybe we should try to make our way down the other side," I suggested. I looked at Rusty and Dave for agreement. They merely stood with their arms wrapped around themselves, shaking in the wind and snow. I didn't know what the other side was like, but I had the feeling it was impassable.

"No," Charlie said. "We make our stand here."

"What are you talking about, Charlie?" I shouted. "They've got guns and they're going to kill us."

"Maybe they'll just take us prisoner again," Dave said hopefully.

"Doubtful," Charlie said.

"I'd rather die than go back to that compound," Rusty said.

I put my nearly frozen arm around her to comfort her. "You may get your wish."

The four men were getting closer and closer as we spoke. I didn't know what sort of plan, if any, Charlie had. I hoped that he would do something quickly. He did. He pulled out his rattle and began chanting. It was a different chant than any I'd learned from Grandma Gladys. I didn't know what it was for, but as Charlie chanted he would nod his head in a particular direction and do part of the chant. Then he would turn to another direction and the chant would change. He ended up doing a three hundred and sixty degree turn as he chanted.

I watched him silently until he was finished, not wanting to disturb his concentration. Then, I asked, "Charlie, what was that?"

"The Four Directions Song," he said quietly. "I was invoking the spirits of the different directions, of the different elements of nature."

"Why?"

"I'm asking them to help work with me."

"I don't understand," I told him. "Work with you for what?"

"You know sound can really shake things up," Charlie said.

"Yeah, I've gathered that from my recent experiences," I replied sarcastically.

"Do you remember the story of Joshua and the walls of Jericho?" Charlie asked in all seriousness.

"Sure," I nodded.

"It's possible that it's a true story," Charlie began. I thought this was a really bad time for a Bible lesson. "His army went around the walls seven times, blowing horns and beating drums. Then, the people gave a great shout, and the walls came down!"

"That's great!" I snickered. "A Bible thumping Indian. Just when I needed one. Are you going to tell me about the glories of heaven next?"

Charlie looked at me and very gently said, "No, Christopher, you don't understand. If they were able to figure out the correct resonant frequency of the wall, they could have caused it to collapse using sound. It's pure physics. What I want to do now is to combine science with spirit. I've asked the energy of the elements to come into my sound."

"Why?" I asked.

Charlie didn't say anything. He stepped forward, and stood at the top of the mountain, as he looked down at the four men who were advancing on us. Then, suddenly, he begin to sing. Only it wasn't really singing. He started making sounds at the very lower end of his vocal range and continued upward until he hit the very top end of his range. He did this twice. It sounded like a siren. At the time, I didn't have a clue why the men below didn't shoot, since at this point, Charlie was not only very visible, he was also very vocal.

The third time Charlie made the siren sound, he stopped at a particular note and held it. He held it for what seemed like an unbelievably long time. Then he took another breath and repeated the note. Suddenly, I could feel things shaking. At first it was subtle. The more Charlie sounded, the more the reverberations grew in intensity until there was a giant roar that filled the air. It was as though the entire mountain was alive with sound.

Somehow, Charlie had been able to figure out the correct resonant frequency of the mountain and set it into vibration. Perhaps it was pure physics, or perhaps the spirits of nature were working with him to create the phenomenon. I guess it really didn't matter how or why. The mountain, with all its snow, was singing with Charlie. It was extraordinary to experience and hear. The sound was almost deafening.

Then came the avalanche. It began just below us, picking up momentum as the snow built up energy and speed. Our four pursuers never had a chance. As soon as they saw the ocean of snow advancing upon them, they turned and began to race down the mountain. They did not get very far. The huge wave of snow passed over them and down into the trees. I could hear the roar of the avalanche. Then, it was deathly quiet.

I turned to Rusty and Dave. None of us said anything. I was numbed by the cold and the snow and by the experience of what had just happened.

"Are they dead?" I asked.

"I don't know," Charlie replied. "It's possible, but I doubt it. I think they're just buried and very disoriented. They should be able to dig themselves out in awhile," he said nodding his head. "Probably."

"But they could be dead," I said again.

"It is possible, Christopher," Charlie said. "I asked the spirits of nature to work with me to help us. I merely provided the sound that they could work through. I can not predict what the action of the spirits will be."

"What a terrible thing," Rusty said.

"There was no choice," Charlie replied. "It was

either us or them. What would you have preferred?"

"It was an act of God," Dave said. "All Charlie did was make a sound."

"It doesn't make any difference," I said. "They could be dead."

"And it's something I'm going to have to live with," Charlie acknowledged. "At least I worked with the nature spirits on this one, not like back in Vietnam."

"I'm sorry," I stated softly. "I know it's all that could be done."

Charlie sighed deeply. Then he began another chant I'd never heard. It was one of the saddest things I had ever experienced, in a language I did not know. I felt like it might have been a prayer for the dead—for the four men that had just been buried by the avalanche, in case they didn't make it. The chant lasted for a couple of minutes. Then Charlie was silent. None of us said a word. The wind whipped through us. The snow continued to cover us. Nobody said anything. We were silent for quite awhile. Finally, Charlie regained his composure and signaled for us to follow him.

Then we headed back down the mountain.

CHAPTER 21

I don't remember much about the journey down. One part of me was doing the levitation mantra and visualizing myself as being light as a feather. Another part of me was again going over the events of the past hour in my head. It didn't seem to make any difference in terms of my concentrating solely on the mantra—it still worked. Perhaps I had reached a point where my consciousness could occupy two spaces simultaneously. This thought didn't make me feel any better.

It was quite probable that the four men who had been pursuing us were not dead. It was possible that they would dig their way out of their snowy burials and begin pursuing us again. This did not make me feel any better either. I have always been an advocate of non-violence, and yet, here I had been partially responsible for what could possibly have been the deaths of four men.

There was no doubt about it. Once I had realized what Charlie was attempting to do with his sounds, I could have stopped him, or at least attempted to stop him. But, I know now that his intention was not to bring death to those who pursued us, but rather to work with the laws of physics and the spirits of nature to merely create an avalanche. It may seem like a subtle difference, but as I meditated on it going down the mountain, I realized that Charlie had been trained to use his hands as lethal weapons. He could have taken the lives of any of the guards that he had physical contact with, but he hadn't. That wasn't his style. With the avalanche, he had let nature have its way.

It was still snowing when we reached the bottom and still light outside. We walked together, very slowly, as we approached the Ranch.

"I hate this Christopher," Rusty said. "I'm not going in."

"We still have to get the Lost Chord back," I reminded her. The brief love and tenderness we'd shown for each other seemed to have faded. I hoped it would come back. I knew we were all tired and numb with cold, and still trying to get a grip on the experience we had just had.

The Ranch seemed silent as we neared it. We didn't see anybody or sense any movement. When we reached the chapel and looked inside, we saw that it was full of people again. They sounded like they were singing hymns.

"What's going on?" I asked.

"Something strange," Charlie observed.

"What could be weirder than what's been going on so far?" I asked. Then, as if in answer, an image of Uncle Jude came into my head. I had forgotten about him until that very moment, but suddenly I remembered. He had been left in the room with the tape of the Lost Chord blasting at him from the cassette player. The automatic reverse might have been broken on the player and not worked even if, as Uncle Jude had thought, we had recorded the Lost Chord on the other side. It hardly mattered. The cassette player would have given him almost forty five minutes worth of sonic revelations before shutting itself off.

"Oh no!" I exclaimed. As I looked more closely into the chapel, I saw the figure of Uncle Jude, lying prone in the center. He didn't look good. In my mind's eye, I saw how he had been found by his confused disciples who had brought him into the chapel in hopes of reviving him.

"Looks like he got a little of his own medicine," Charlie said.

"We've have to help him," I said.

"Let me go in!" Rusty insisted. Despite her prior experiences with Uncle Jude, she was still willing to assist him. She was an amazing woman. "If those people see you, they might tear you apart," she said to me and Charlie.

"Agreed," Charlie and I replied.

"I'll go with you," Dave called to Rusty. "I've learned some CPR. Maybe that'll help." Together they walked silently and slowly into the chapel.

It's weird the way my enhanced psychic abilities will click in sometimes and other times give me nothing. For some reason, at this very moment in time and space, I was getting a very accurate and in depth reading on Uncle Jude. He had indeed received forty-five minutes exposure to the Lost Chord before he was discovered by one of his devotees. It was more then even he could take.

The Chord created a gateway to other dimensions. The difficulty about it was returning from the other dimensions. Even my brief 5 minute exposure to the Lost Chord frequencies, which had put me out of my body for an hour and a half, had made me immediately want to use the Chord again. In Jude Primer's case, he was still out of his body and not likely to re-enter the physical plane any time soon. Some aspect of his psyche was trapped in another dimension. I hoped it was a nice one.

I doubted that he would ever return.

Charlie and I stood at the back of the chapel while Rusty and Dave examined Uncle Jude. No one stopped them, nor did anyone notice us at the back. After a minute, Charlie and I slowly made our way to the other door which lead to the main entrance of the Ranch. We waited inside the glass walkway for Rusty and Dave to come out. They did so a few minutes later.

"He looks catatonic," Dave said.

Rusty nodded glumly. "He's gone," she said. "His eyes are open, but he's not conscious of anything." She turned to me and buried her face in my shoulder, sobbing. "I suppose I should feel satisfied at this, but what's happened to him shouldn't happen to anyone."

I gently soothed her. "I know," I said, trying to comfort her. "We warned him about what could happen. In fact," I added, "that was supposed to have happened to Charlie and me."

I don't know if the thought made her any happier, but Rusty looked up at me. "Really? How did you get away?"

"Later!" I told her. "Right now, despite all that has happened, we have to find all copies of the Lost Chord and take them back."

"Agreed," Charlie said. Rusty and Dave nodded.

For some reason I felt that I was in control again, perhaps for the first time in quite awhile. Maybe control is just an illusion. It didn't matter—we had another task to perform before we could leave the Ranch. "Charlie, you go with Dave and retrieve the tape player that we left in the interrogation room. Please make sure that someone didn't press play again before you enter the room."

"Don't worry," Charlie answered, pulling out the ear

plugs. "I still have these."

"As though you need them," I replied cynically, "Master of sound that you are."

"Rusty," I said firmly. "You come with me. We're going back into Uncle Jude's studio. We have to make sure we take all the disks, tapes, and anything else that might have your Lost Chord frequencies on it."

Rusty nodded. Then we split up. Rusty and I made our way back into Uncle Jude's recording studio. Almost immediately, we found a duplicate disk of Rusty's Lost Chord frequencies that Uncle Jude had made. Then, we found a reel of tape that had been conveniently marked "Jude's Magic Music". It contained the millisecond bursts of the Lost Chord that had been used in the chapel. The sound was no longer being piped into the chapel, but the tape machine with the reel was still turning when we went into the studio. I hit the stop button and removed the 10 inch reel from the machine. Rusty found a bulk tape demagnetizer. She ran it across "Jude's Magic Music", silencing it forever.

"Is that it?" I asked.

"Keep looking," Rusty responded. "There's one more."

We rummaged through other assorted tapes and disks in the studio, and finally found the original disk of the Lost Chord that had been duplicated and stolen from Rusty. There was nothing else. Satisfied that we had found all of Jude's copies of the Chord, Rusty turned to me, nodding her head. "I think that's it, Christopher!"

I looked around the studio one last time. "This is such a beautiful place, with such incredible possibilities. Too bad he was trying to use it for evil."

"Maybe I'm the one responsible for all of this,"

Rusty said sadly. "If I hadn't created the Lost Chord....".

I didn't want to get into a philosophical discussion at that time. "Later!" I said. "Let's just get out of here."

Rusty nodded and followed me out.

The Ranch was deserted except for the two of us. There were no guards around. Perhaps there were no guards left. Everyone else was in the chapel, praying for Uncle Jude. I sincerely hoped they were successful. I agreed with Rusty—nobody should be left in that condition. I didn't know what would happen to Jude's followers now that their great leader had taken a fall. It was possible that he would recover. It was possible that they would find someone else to lead them. It was more likely, however, that in a short time, they would all abandon the Ranch. In my mind's eye, I saw a "For Sale" on the gate where the "No Trespassing" sign had been. Maybe it was a premonition. Maybe not.

Charlie and Dave were waiting outside for us in the Bronco. It hadn't been disturbed since we first arrived hours before. The engine was running. Charlie was sitting at the steering wheel. Dave waved to us as we came down the stairs and lifted up the ghetto blaster for us to see.

Rusty and I climbed in the back seat. I was so exhausted, I was glad to have Charlie driving. I didn't know where his energy came from. Perhaps he was able to tap into some inexhaustible source. I didn't know. I didn't care. I just wanted to go home.

"Home, James!" I said.

"Yes sir!" Charlie answered. He put the Bronco in gear and headed down the dirt road that led to freedom.

"I'm so tired, Christopher," Rusty said snuggling against me.

I felt the electricity we had briefly shared on the mountain return. Despite my exhaustion, my body was tingling. "Would you like to come sleep at my place?" I asked timidly. I didn't want to offend her. It was the last thing on my mind. And yet, once again, I knew I was in love with her.

"Nothing would please me more!" she whispered in my ear. Then she kissed me on the cheek. Then she fell asleep.

I dozed on the way down the mountain to Boulder. During my sleep, Shamael, the Angel of Sound came to me.

"You have done well, Christopher Shade," the angel said.

I was in the temple, as usual. I guess that was our preordained meeting spot. "Where were you when I needed you?" I asked.

The angel laughed. "We have been with you throughout this time, as we are always with you. Who do you think carried you up that mountain?"

"Is there anything more that I should do?"

"Many things," Shamael said. "But we can not interfere. We trust that you will make the right decisions. You are in the process of learning. Remember, we will always be there if you need us."

Then things began to spiral and suddenly the car stopped in front of my house. Dave had already been dropped off.

"Mind if I spend the night?" Charlie asked.

"No problem," I said. "I have a great couch in the living room."

Charlie and I helped Rusty sleep walk her way into my apartment. We put her down on my bed. Then I walked into the living room with Charlie. "Is there anything else you need my friend?" I asked.

Charlie smiled. "No, I'm fine Christopher, but I think you'd better get some sleep."

"I want to thank you for all your help, Charlie Singing Eagle," I said. Then I gave him a warm hug and staggered off to bed.

I was so tired, I could barely kick my shoes off. I crawled into bed with Rusty. I visualized waking her and making mad passionate love until the dawn arose. It was a lovely thought and it lasted about 30 seconds. Then I fell asleep.

CHAPTER 22

I had no dreams that night, at least none that I can remember. But when Rusty and I woke up we did make mad passionate love. It didn't last until the dawn arose, as I had envisioned before I fell asleep, because we didn't get up until around 8 that morning. I was delighted to find that Rusty's feelings for me had not changed now that she had a good night's sleep. I was also glad to find that the feelings I had for her were found in my heart and not primarily in my lower chakra.

We cuddled and talked and made love once more before rising for the morning. I had been surprised to discover that she had been attracted to me since we had first met. It had just been my attitude that had put her off. It's amazing what an experience with an archangel and a medicine woman can do for one's consciousness. At one point, the conversation turned very serious.

"Christopher," she asked, "What am I going to do about the Lost Chord?"

I looked lovingly into her beautiful green eyes. "What do you want to do, Rusty? We've got it back now. You can do anything you like. It is, after all, your creation."

"But it's so dangerous!" Rusty bitterly acknowledged.

"No kidding," I said.

"Do you think I should destroy it?"

"I don't know," I answered as truthfully as I could.

"What would you do?" Rusty asked.

"I don't know," I repeated. I didn't. On one hand, what Rusty had created could be an invaluable tool that had the potential of raising the consciousness of humankind. On the other hand, as we had found out, the Lost Chord had the potential of being an extraordinary weapon of power and control.

"Maybe I should wipe out the disks and the program. That would take care of everything," Rusty said, nodding to herself.

"That would do it, I'm sure," I answered. "But it does represent years of work. I think the Lost Chord truly has the possibility of being used for good."

"How?" Rusty asked, sitting up in bed.

I shrugged my shoulders. "I'm not sure right now. We've only seen it's destructive use, but I'm sure it could be used for good. I don't know if I'd destroy it yet."

"I've been thinking a lot about this, Christopher, ever since you freed me from the chapel. I just don't think the world is ready for the power it's able to channel."

"You could be right," I told her. "But I sure would like to try it again."

Just then there was a knock on the bedroom door. "Coffee's ready!" Charlie's voice boomed from the other side.

"Thanks," I said. Then I turned to Rusty, "Do you drink coffee?"

"Love it," she said. She kissed me on the cheek. "Mind if I take a shower?"

"No problem, my sweets. I'll take one after you. I've also got some clothes you can borrow if you like. Want me to get them for you?"

"That would be lovely," Rusty said. At that moment, I thought about asking her to live with me. In my mind's eye, I saw that it was a good possibility. I figured we needed to decide what to do about the Lost Chord first.

I stood up and went to my closet. A minute later, I returned with a towel and some fresh clothes which I handed to her.

"Thanks," Rusty said, kissing me again on the cheek. Then she disappeared into the bathroom.

I dressed, slipping on my old clothes with the idea of changing after my shower. Then, I stepped into the kitchen. Charlie had brewed some coffee. He seemed to be handy in all different situations. He handed me a cup. "Cream and sugar?" he asked.

"Thanks," I said, holding up my hand. "I'll add it myself," which I did.

I sat in the kitchen sipping the coffee, thinking. Charlie sat across the kitchen table from me, also deeply involved in thought.

"Do you think Rusty should destroy the Lost Chord?" I asked him.

Charlie looked at me like I was crazy. "What? After all I've gone through with you, you're thinking of destroying it before I try it? I have to see what this fuss is all about."

"It's addictive, Charlie. It can be a narcotic and we've seen what overexposure to it can do."

Charlie nodded, "Yes, we have. "

"Besides, it's not natural—it's human made," I said, still thinking out loud. "It's a powerful technological tool that can be used by anyone lacking the spiritual discipline to know its full effect."

"So, I don't get to try it?" Charlie said.

"I didn't say that," I replied. "I just don't know. It's up to Rusty. I think she wants to destroy it."

"Did you speak to your angel about this?"

I shrugged my shoulders. "The angel is not allowed to interfere with human decisions. He can only guide. He said I would know what to do."

"So?"

"I just don't know, Charlie."

Rusty came out of the bathroom, wearing the tee shirt, jeans and flannel shirt I'd given her. She looked radiant.

"What are you talking about?" she asked, as Charlie handed her a cup of coffee.

"The Lost Chord, what else?" I answered.

"I'm going to destroy it," Rusty stated. "There's no other choice."

"Charlie wants to try it," I said, trying to give her an argument. "We owe him that much."

"Christopher," Rusty said firmly, "Go take your shower. I'll talk to Charlie."

I did as I was commanded. I've always liked strong women. Besides, I really needed a shower. When I had freshened up and was dressed, I walked back into the kitchen. "Shower, Charlie?" I asked. He was sitting on the couch which had been his bed.

"Lost Chord, Christopher," he said, pointing to the portable cassette player which we had brought in the night before, along with my guitar.

"I found a set of headphones to use," Rusty said. They were connected to the stereo unit.

"Okay," I said, throwing my hands up. I didn't know what to say. "Just five minutes worth, like the rest of us."

"Whatever you want," Charlie answered. He put on the headphones.

Rusty hit the play button on the cassette player. Almost immediately Charlie was out. After 5 minutes, she hit the stop button. I turned to her, "You know, you might be able to make some serious money with this. Open up Lost Chord Parlors! Get a bunch of beds, have people lie on them and then play the Lost Chord for a couple of minutes. An hour later you can get a whole new group of people. You can charge twenty-five dollars a trip and really rake in the bucks."

Rusty looked at me, wondering if I was serious or not. "I've thought of it, Christopher," she replied. "But you know, someone would try to steal the frequencies again, or the government would seize the Lost Chord for its own use. I can't decide what I should do."

"Maybe you should just lay low with it. You know, don't tell anyone else about the frequencies. Take all the copies of the tapes and disks and computer program and put them in a safety deposit box or somewhere else safe." I took her hand as we watched Charlie. "There must be some way the Lost Chord can be used positively. It would be a great loss if we finally understood how that was possible and didn't have the frequencies."

Rusty nodded. "That's not a bad idea, but I wouldn't want the responsibility of having the key to that safety deposit box you're talking about."

"Maybe I could hold it," I suggested. Then another idea struck. "Or maybe we could place all the Lost Chords in a place where no one would ever find them."

"What are you talking about?" Rusty asked.

Just then Charlie began to stir. I looked at my wristwatch. It had been only fifteen minutes since he first began the program. Rusty's mouth dropped open in disbelief as Charlie opened his eyes.

"Wow!" he said. "What a trip!"

"My sentiments exactly," I affirmed. "But what are you doing back so soon? Everyone else who has tried the Lost Chord has been out for at least an hour."

"Oh," Charlie said nonchalantly, "I could have stayed out longer. I was having this great conversation with Black Elk. He's one of my guides you know. But I knew we had business to take care of, so I came back."

"How?" I asked, trying to comprehend the situation.

"The grounding mantra," Charlie replied. "This Lost Chord creates a wonderful space, but it's really nothing new for me. Just a different way of approaching it."

"Then how come I was able to contact the Angel of Sound on my journey?"

"It was new for you, Christopher," Charlie told me. "You've made contact with him since then, haven't you."

"Yes, indeed," I affirmed.

"Without the Lost Chord, right?"

"That's true," I answered.

"Then it's really not as dangerous as we thought," Rusty chimed in.

Charlie shook his head and laughed. "Oh, it's dangerous all right. Very dangerous. Especially for the uninitiated. You have to remember, I've had some training in this journeying work before. Don't forget what happened to Uncle Jude."

"I wonder what has become of him and his followers,"

I mused sadly.

"We may never find out," Charlie said. "Then again, it might be in the headlines of today's paper."

"Do you think so?" Rusty asked. Charlie merely shrugged his shoulders.

I grabbed my coat and handed Rusty hers. "Come on," I said. "We've got some work to do."

"Where are we going, Christopher?" she asked.

I opened the portable cassette player and removed the Lost Chord tape. Then, I patted my pocket to make sure that all the disks that we had retrieved from Uncle Jude were still there.

"Trust me," I said. Then the three of us headed out the door.

CHAPTER 23

First, we drove to Rusty's condo to pick up the remaining copies of the Lost Chord. Rusty was able to remove information from her computer's hard drive onto a disk, clearing out the information that was there. That took about ten minutes. She handed the computer disks to me. I put them in my pocket.

Next, we went to pick up Dave. I had called him from Rusty's and, remarkably, he was ready by the time we arrived. I was driving this time, with Charlie in the front seat. Dave joined Rusty in the back seat.

"What's up, Shade?" he asked sleepily.

"I thought you'd want to join us for this last little adventure," I told him. I said no more, and we proceeded to our next destination which was a Quik Mart convenience store.

At the store I bought *The Daily Camera* and quickly scanned it, looking for something about our encounter in the mountains. There was nothing about Uncle Jude or the Ranch on the front page, or anywhere else I looked. I handed the paper to Rusty. "See if you can find anything," I suggested. She nodded and began thumbing through the paper.

My final stop in Boulder was McGuckins, a huge hardware store where you can find almost anything in the world. It does have hardware, but also sports equipment, music supplies, toys for kids and what not. I found a small, waterproof plastic lined container which I bought.

Once in the car, I switched places with Charlie. We headed up the Canyon towards Nederland. Our destination was Grandma Gladys Goodnight's. She had played an important role in this adventure, and I knew we all needed to see her.

Rusty had found a small quarter column article hidden in the paper with the header, "Local Guru Suffers Stroke". It told of how Uncle Jude had been rushed to Boulder Community hospital last night in a comatose condition which paramedics perceived of as a stroke. It made no mention of anything else except to say that Jude Primer was a local musician with a following, and that he had established a community in Gold Hill.

"Not much to sink your teeth into," I said, after listening to Rusty read the article.

"Maybe there'll be follow-ups," Dave said.

"I wouldn't count on that," Charlie stated. "I have a feeling that the Ranch community will last a little while longer without Jude to lead them. But, it's been my understanding that a cult without a leader isn't much of a cult. Cults depend very much on the charisma and power of an individual leader. Without that, the energy collapses."

I remembered my vision of the "For Sale" sign on the electrified fence, but said nothing. There had been too many things that had occurred over the past few days for me to be sure of anything. I couldn't even help Rusty decide what to do with the Lost Chord. That was why we were on our way to see Grandma Gladys.

It had stopped snowing during the night. The journey up the mountain was not dangerous and the scenery was beautiful. Everything was covered with a rich, wonderful whiteness that seemed to glow in the warmth of the Colorado sunshine. The higher we went up into the mountains, the more beautiful it became. Once we arrived at our destination, it felt like magic. The pine trees at Grandma Gladys' place looked serene and peaceful in the snow.

"Isn't it gorgeous, Christopher?" Rusty said, as we got out of the Bronco and began walking toward Gladys' cabin.

"It sure is, Rusty," I said. "And it's good to be alive." It was, too.

She took my left arm as we walked. In my right hand I carried the waterproof case I had just bought.

We had all been fairly quiet on the way up the mountain, still processing the events of the days before. Now, finally we were at Grandma Gladys'. I was excited to be able to introduce her to Rusty and Dave. I had told them a bit about her during our drive that day, but I knew words could not do her justice. I really wanted them to meet her in person. I had the feeling she had something more to share with me, perhaps with all of us.

As we approached her little cabin, Gladys was standing at the door. "I knew you were coming," she said with a smile. She hugged each of us as we went in: first Charlie, then Dave, then Rusty, and finally me. "I guess you learned to walk with the sound of the Great Spirit after all, Christopher," she said as she warmly embraced me.

"I guess I did, ma'am," I said shyly. The power and radiance of this petite woman still overwhelmed me. "I wanted my friends to meet you. And I need to talk with you."

"Well, I've brewed some coffee. You and your friends take a seat and we'll talk," Gladys said, ushering me into the cabin. We all took seats by the fireplace. Grandma Gladys had arranged four chairs beside her own.

I formally introduced Rusty and Dave, and then began filling Gladys in on all the events of the day before. I think it wasn't really necessary. She kept nodding at everything I told her, as though she had been there with us. As a matter of fact, in a way, I think she was. I had felt her presence since I had first met her. It wasn't just through using the mantras she had taught me—it was something intangible, but nevertheless real.

Finally, we began to discuss the real reason I had come to see her. "So, you see Gladys," I said, holding up the waterproof container that held all the disks and tapes of the Lost Chord, "This is all that remains of those frequencies. I don't know what to do with them. I just can't make the decision. You say the word, and I'll throw them into the fire."

"Now, why would you want to do that, boy?" Grandma Gladys said with a laugh. "Your lady friend, Rusty, has spent years creating those sounds."

Rusty beamed at the mention of her name. Then she got somber and told Gladys, "But they seem to be used only for evil."

"Honey," Gladys began, "life and the universe are a constant flow of energy, of the struggle between what some people call good and evil, dark and light. It's just energy. You had the experience of your Lost Chord being applied in a certain way." She shook her head. "Whether we like it or not, this Lost Chord of yours has now manifested here on the planet Earth. If we throw that box in the fire right now, I can almost guarantee that somebody else will create it soon. Maybe sooner than you think. That's just the way it is here," Gladys chuckled. "It's better that you, who have some understanding of it, be the guardian of the energies. Especially with your friend, Christopher, to help you."

"Would you take care of this container and its contents for awhile?" I asked, handing Gladys the waterproof container with the Lost Chord disks and tapes in it.

Gladys smiled. "Sure child. I'll put them somewhere special. Whenever you want them, they'll be here."

"Thank you," I said most graciously.

"No, thank you, Christopher," she said. "You have worked hard and well on this. You are to be thanked."

Rusty, who was sitting next to me, took my hand and smiled at me. For the moment at least, all was well with the world. Then more thoughts of the day before came rushing at me.

"I can't help thinking about what happened to Uncle Jude and the men the avalanche buried," I told her. "I hate violence."

"Christopher, you were not responsible for what happened to those men. You may not fully understand it now, but you were acting as an agent of the forces of the Great Spirit. You didn't make Uncle Jude try to destroy you with that tape of the Lost Chord, and you didn't make those men chase you up that mountain. Charlie here," she pointed to Singing Eagle, sitting next to her, "was only calling on the Spirits of the mountains and to help you escape from being killed. It was not his intention that those men might get injured, but it was part of the Divine Plan."

"Divine Plan?" I asked.

"Christopher," Gladys said, "You've been going through a training on many different planes that I know, for sure, you haven't completely assimilated. That's good. Because it's been an advanced training—one that should have taken a lot longer than you were given. But, you were needed to do a very special job. And you'll be needed again."

"Again?" I repeated. "Please Grandma Gladys, once was enough."

"That big old archangel behind you is laughing, Christopher," Gladys said, pointing behind me. I looked around and naturally saw nothing. "He knows what's in store for you, but he's not saying." She giggled.

"Oh great!" I said. "I just want to go back to playing some blues."

"You'll do that, too, boy," Gladys replied. "As I think you're supposed to be doing some playing tonight."

Dave and I looked at each other. She was right. "Sound check," I mouthed to Dave.

"I know it's time that you need to leave," Gladys said. "But remember, Christopher and Rusty and Dave, if you ever need my help, I'll be here."

The three of us stood up and thanked Grandma Gladys. Charlie was staying at the cabin with his teacher. He rose from his chair and gave me a mighty hug. "May you walk the good road!" he said.

"Come by the Dugout next time you dream me," I told him.

Charlie laughed, "I hope it'll be before that."

"Don't worry boys," Grandma Gladys said. "Your paths will cross sooner than you think."

Then, after our goodbyes, we were off. It was two hours before sound check, and this time I wanted to be there early. I drove down the mountain slowly, still admiring the beauty that the storm had left. Then, I dropped Dave off at his place, and Rusty off at her place. She had promised to make it to the gig. I told her I would be counting the minutes until I saw her again. It was true.

I had about an hour at home before I needed to leave for sound check. I sat on my couch, trying to process the experiences of the last few days. I knew I was a changed person, though how much I had changed would not become immediately apparent. I contemplated Gladys' remark about my being needed again. I was serious when I told her that once was enough.

I had learned an incredible amount about the extraordinary power of sound to create, change, and shift reality. I have passed what I can on to you. Sound has the ability to do amazing things. I didn't realize at the time, that this was only the beginning of my experiences with sound and the spiritual. There would be more. Much more. I think if I'd known what was in store for me, I might have packed up my guitar and headed back to Boston.

Instead, I picked up my guitar and headed out to the Dugout. The Lost Chord was safe. I was in love. I knew it was going to be a great gig that night. Somehow, as I was leaving my house, I thought I caught the image out of the corner of my eye of a huge shimmering being with multi-colored wings. He was standing in my living room, a look of ancient wisdom upon his face. He was laughing.

Christopher Shade will return in
The Tibetan Blues

SUGGESTED READING

Author's note: While *The Lost Chord* is a work of fiction, much of the information about sound contained within it is based upon fact. For those readers who wish to further expand their interest in sound, I have compiled the following reading list. The awareness of sound and music as therapeutic and transformation tools is growing rapidly. As such, there are more and more books manifesting on the subject. The following are some of my favorites. — JG

Andrews, Ted, *Sacred Sounds* (Llewellyn, 1992).

Beaulieu, John, *Music And Sound In The Healing Arts* (Station Hill, 1987).

Berendt, J.E., *Nada Brahma: The World is Sound* (Destiny, 1987)

Campbell, Don, *The Roar Of Silence* (Quest, 1990)

——, *Music: Physician For Times To Come* (Quest, 1990)

DeMohan, Elias, *The Harmonics Of Sound, Color And Vibration*, (DeVorss, 1994)

Gardner, Kay, *Sounding The Inner Landscape* (Caduceus, 1990)

Gardner, Joy, *The Healing Voice* (Crossing Press, 1993)

Garfield, Laeh Maggie, *Sound Medicine* (Celestial Arts, 1987)

Gass, Robert, *Chanting* (Broadway, 1999)

Goldman, Jonathan, *Healing Sounds,* (Element, 1996)

——, *Shifting Frequencies,* (Light Technology, 1998)

Halpern, Steven and Louis Savary, *Sound Health,* (Harper & Row, 1985)

Hamel, Peter Michael, *Through Music To The Self,* Shambhala, 1978)

Kenyon, Tom, *Brain States,* (United States, 1994)

Keyes, Elizabeth Laurel, *Toning: The Creative Power Of The Voice,* (DeVorss, 1973)

Khan, Hazrat Inayat, *The Mysticism Of Sound,* (Barry& Rockcliff, 1962)

Maman, Fabian, *The Role Of Music In The 21st Century,* (Tama-Do, 1998)

McClellan, Randall, *The Healing Forces Of Music: History, Theory And Practice* (Element, 1988)

Rael, Joseph, *Being And Vibration,* (Council Oak Books, 1993)

Rudyhar, Dane, *The Magic Of Tone And The Art Of Music,* (Shambhala, 1983)

Tomatis, Alfred A., *The Conscious Ear* (Station Hill, 1991)

White, Harvey and Donald, *Physics of Music* (Holt, Rinehart & Winston, 1980)

ABOUT JONATHAN GOLDMAN

Jonathan Goldman is an authority on sound healing and a pioneer in the field of harmonics. He has studied with masters of sound from both the scientific and spiritual traditions and has been empowered by the Chant Master of the Dalai Lama's Drepung Loseling Monastery to teach Tibetan Overtone chanting.

His first book, *Healing Sounds: The Power of Harmonics* from Element, is now in its second edition and has been translated into numerous languages. It is considered a landmark in the sound healing arena. His second book, *Shifting Frequencies,* has recently been published by Light Technology and contains new cutting edge information on the transformational uses of sound and other vibrational modalities. His highly acclaimed recordings include: *Dolphin Dreams, Gateways: Drumming and Chanting, Trance Tara* and the best selling *Chakra Chants.*

Jonathan is the director of the Sound Healers Association and president of Spirit Music in Boulder, Colorado. He travels throughout the world empowering others with the ability to create and use healing and transformational sounds.

Before his sojourn into sound healing in 1980, Jonathan was a rock n' roll musician. He graduated from Boston University with a degree in film making and holds an M.A. from Lesley College in Independent Study of the Uses of Sound and Music for Healing. *The Lost Chord* is Jonathan's first published novel.

To contact Jonathan Goldman:
email: soundheals@aol.com
telephone: (303) 443-8181
fax: (303) 443-6023
mail: P.O. Box 2240
Boulder CO 80306 USA
Visit our website at: http://www.healingsounds.com

TRAININGS WITH JONATHAN GOLDMAN

HEALING SOUNDS INTENSIVE
This is a nine day long training in the beautiful mountains outside of Boulder with Chant Master Jonathan Goldman. It is a step- by-step process of learning to use sound for vibrational repatterning and alignment. Combining over 20 years of experience in researching, exploring, and teaching the uses of sound as a healing and transformational modality, Jonathan has created a program rich in experiences and information. It will cover the latest scientific material on sonics as well as bringing you time honored sacred sound from different traditions. You will learn in a special atmosphere of serenity and love, with a select group of explorers of sound. You will discover how to use sound as a healing and transformation modality, to enrich your life and work. Areas of focus include: Vowels as Mantras, Pythagorean Intervals, Psycho-Acoustics & the Brain, Bija Mantras, Light and Sound, Sonic Yoga of Listening, Sacred Geometry and Sound, Song of the Soul, Chakra Chants, Vocal Harmonics, Angel of Sound Initiation, Creating Group Merkabahs, Chanting and Drumming, Sound and Crystals, Sonic Shamanism, Toning and Overtoning,

HEALING SOUNDS SEMINARS
These are week-end long seminar created to give sonic initiatory experiences to those who attend. The first level of the seminar includes: Vowels As Mantras, Vocal Harmonics, Overtoning and much more! There are three levels to the HEALING SOUNDS SEMINAR. Each level is given over an entire week-end and includes experiential exercises in sacred sound.

CORRESPONDENCE COURSE
Discover the mysteries of sound healing in a semester length independent study program that you can pursue in your own own. The Correspondence Course was designed to develop your ability to use your own voice for self transformation and healing. Experience the benefits of sound for yourself.

MATERIALS FROM JONATHAN GOLDMAN

BOOKS

HEALING SOUNDS   **HS1 $17.00**
The first and only book to share the extraordinary power of harmonics to heal and transform. Discover the mystical and sacred traditions of sound and experience how vocal harmonics will benefit your life. Includes information on the ancient mystery schools, shamanic, kabbalistic and Tibetan traditions. Now in its second edition, this book is considered a landmark in the sound healing arena.

SHIFTING FREQUENCIES   **SF2 $15.00**
A compilation of Jonathan's columns from *"Sedona Emergence"*, this book contains cutting edge information on how sound and other vibrational modalities, including light, sacred geometry and crystals can be used for healing and self-transformation. Lots of illustrations. Provides a new understanding about frequency and our ability to create change.

MUSIC

DOLPHIN DREAMS CD: DD3 $16.00 Cassette: DD3C $11.00
A unique sound experience with ocean, heart beat, choral voices and dolphins. Organic sounds create a soothing psycho-acoustic sonic environment with many different applications. Truly a new sound experience. This recording has become one of the most popular on the planet for both the birthing experience and for deep relaxation.

TRANCE TARA   **CD: TT4 $16 Cassette: TT4C $11.00**
A musical offering to Tara, Tibetan Goddess of Compassion. Two side long pieces of extraordinary energy featuring male and female choruses, Tibetan Overtone Chanting, Singing Bowls, Bells and powerful tribal drumming. Great for movement, meditation and trance dance.

GATEWAYS   CD: G5 $16.00   Cassette: G5C $11.00
Six sacred chants with drumming from different traditions, including Native American, Tibetan, Hindu and Hebrew. Women and children love this music too.

CHAKRA CHANTS   CD: CC6 $16.00
Combines the seven sacred Vowels with Bija Mantras from the Vedic tradition with Pythagorean tunings, Elemental and Shabd Yoga Sounds, Male and Female Choral Voices, Sound Current Toning and more! For an extraordinary hour long psycho sonic experience of meditation and deep sound healing. It initiates a new level of therapeutic uses of sound.

ANGEL OF SOUND   Cassette: AS7 $11.00
A sonic environment to invoke the energies of Shamael, Angel of Sound. Features: Tibetan Overtone Chanting, bowls, bells, Native American Flute, vocal harmonics, drums. Powerful.

SONG OF SARASWATI   Cassette: SS8 $11.00
A chant with music to invoke the Hindu Goddess of Music. Features: male and female voices, vocal harmonics tambura, Tibetan bells and more. Beautiful and hypnotic.

HERMETIC HARMONICS   Cassette: HH9 $11.00
Features: overtone chanting and Tibetan bells multi-tracked to create a powerful trance inducing, meditative experience. Great for ritual, healing or for a background for toning.

HARMONIC JOURNEYS   Cassette: HJ10 $13.00
An instructional tape with exercises designed to accompany *Healing Sounds*. Side One features "Vowels as Mantras". Side Two features "The Fundamentals of Vocal Harmonics".

CELESTIAL REALMS   Cassette: LL 11 $11.00
Goldman performs with renown musician Laraaji. Together they create extraordinary hypnotic music on synthesizer, guitar, bells and zither. It will relax and entrance you.

THE LOST CHORD (Late 1999) **CD: LC12 $16.00**
The book is fiction. This recording is not. Combining his knowledge of psycho-acoustics and sacred sound, Jonathan Goldman has created a safe, soothing and beautiful hour long recording designed to relax even the most stressed out listener. Contains Tibetan Overtone Chanting, mantras from different traditions, sonic entrainment frequencies, sacred ratios and much more.

TOOLS

PYTHAGOREAN TUNING FORKS **PF12 $39.00**
This set of two aluminum tuning forks is cut to the sacred ratio of the perfect fifth. They vibrate at a ratio of 2:3. Their frequencies are C 256 and G 384. The intervals that are created when these two tuning forks sound together creates a deeply balancing and relaxing response in the listener. Great for stress reduction, energy and body work.

D n' A# TUNING FORKS **DA13 $39.00**
This set of two tuning forks create a new ratio that has not manifested on the planet for many a millennium. They vibrate at a ratio of 8:13. Their frequencies are D 288 and A# 468. They are said to balance the brain and the chakras and open up interdimensional gateways. Encode the Light! Feel the spirals and hear the angels calling you when you use these forks.

CRYSTAL RESONATORS **CR14 $20.00**
Strike this tuning fork on a hard surface and bring it near a quartz crystal or yourself. A sub-harmonic of the actual frequencies of quartz. It clears and cleanses crystals and human. Said to be wonderful in the Great Pyramid.

For a complete catalog, contact Spirit Music at:
email: soundheals@aol.com
telephone: (303) 443-8181 or (800) 246-9764
fax: (303) 443-6023
mail: P.O. Box 2240
Boulder CO 80306 USA
Visit our website at: http://www.healingsounds.com

ORDERING PAGE

Please write item number and price   _____

(include additional page if necessary)   _____

_____

_____

_____

_____

Subtotal   _____

Postage & Handling $3.00 for first item.   _____

$1.00 for each additional item.   _____

Colorado residents add 7% sales tax.   _____

Overseas Airmail add $4.00 ea. CASS/CD.   _____

Overseas Airmail add $6.00 ea. Book.   _____

Total enclosed. In U.S. dollars: _____

Make checks payable to: SPIRIT MUSIC
PO Box 2240, Boulder CO 80306 USA
Ph: (303) 443-8181   Fax: (303) 443-6023

1-800-246-9764 orders only (allow 2 to 4 weeks for delivery)

❏ VISA ❏ MASTERCARD Expiration date_____

CARD #_____

Print Name:_____

Signature: _____

Phone number: _____

Address:_____

City:_____

State: _____ Zip:_____ Country: _____

❏ Send info on Correspondence Course, Sound Intensives, or other Jonathan Goldman workshops and events